AF580743

THE ASSASSIN'S GUIDE TO DATING

The Assassin's Guide to Dating

Natalie C. Parker

Candlewick Press

This is a work of fiction. Names, characters, places, and incidents are either products of the author's imagination or, if real, are used fictitiously.

Copyright © 2026 by Natalie C. Parker

All rights reserved. No part of this book may be reproduced, transmitted, or stored in an information retrieval system in any form or by any means, graphic, electronic, or mechanical, including photocopying, taping, and recording, without prior written permission from the publisher. Additionally, no part of this book may be used or reproduced in any manner for the purpose of training artificial intelligence technologies or systems, nor for text and data mining.

First edition 2026

Library of Congress Control Number: 2026934569
ISBN 978-1-5362-4329-1

SHD 31 30 29 28 27 26
10 9 8 7 6 5 4 3 2 1

Printed in Chelsea, MI, USA

This book was typeset in Palatino Pro.

Candlewick Press
99 Dover Street
Somerville, Massachusetts 02144

www.candlewick.com

EU Authorized Representative: HackettFlynn Ltd,
36 Cloch Choirneal, Balrothery,
Co. Dublin, K32 C942, Ireland.
EU@walkerpublishinggroup.com

THIS ONE IS FOR *MIRIAM*,
WHO SPARKED THIS STORY
WITH A SINGLE QUESTION.

They say that bombshells die young, that most of us burn out before we have a chance to really live, and the only thing we're any good at is dying. I have wanted to prove them wrong my entire life, but I'm starting to wonder if maybe they're right after all.

My father was a bombshell, like me. In my memory, he was soft-spoken and studious, not the raging alcoholic people say he was. I have more memories of finding him in the little corner of the living room he called his office, researching something—I'm not sure what—with a kind of fevered intensity, his nose so close to the computer screen he nearly bumped it. He never made the fonts larger, no matter how many times Sage and I showed him how.

I've never been able to reconcile that image of my father with the one from the day he lost control of his talent and killed a dozen people in the Power and Light district. They say he was drinking—drunk—but I never saw him have more than a beer or two at home. They say he was furious, but I never saw him lose his temper. Not even at Sage, and if either of us was going to push him over the edge, she'd be the first to admit that it would have been her.

I don't remember where I was when I heard my father had died. Sage says we were in school, and she's usually right about things like that. All I remember is that one day our lives were fairly normal for kids with talents, and the next I was the pariah of St. Isidor's High. One day, I had friends who sat with me at lunch and stressed about what we would wear to the gala when it was our turn, and the next I was alone. But most of all I remember that from one day to the next, I went from thinking the world was mostly good, to knowing it was not.

We learned about the traitor bounty after—that he'd been too reckless too many times. When he lost control in broad daylight, that was enough to put a mark on his head. I still don't know if his death was intentional or not, but since it occurred under the terms of an official bounty, it was all legit and legal in the eyes of Underhill. And expected in the eyes of everyone else.

Bombshells were named for the explosive power that lives inside us and the way it looks when we use our talent, when we become fissures of heat and light, a bomb exploding in slow motion. I've worked all my life to combat the assumption that we are volatile—that *I*, as the daughter of Bruce Morgan, am volatile—but it seems that when my teacher and mentor,

Ms. Jones, attacked Boss Acosta and nearly took out half of Underhill in the process, all my work was forgotten.

After two months, in the quiet, early morning halls of Underhill, I can still feel the echoing shock waves of that blast. It's typical for Underhill to be sparsely populated at this time of day, but there are more people dressed in Executive gold than I usually see. A few of them look surprised to see me and give me a much wider berth than is necessary or polite, but most hurry past hoping I won't notice that they put on a little extra speed. As if I'll explode before they can reach a minimum safe distance.

I resist the urge to grit my teeth and raise my chin instead.

One of the first things Ms. Jones ever said to me was "When they call us bombshell, they are telling themselves a story of who we will be. Who they fear we will be. You must remember that it is not the whole story. You are more than a bombshell, Lila. You are a force, one that can be harnessed."

She believed that she could change the way people perceived bombshells, and she pursued that belief the way she did everything else, with unwavering devotion and confidence.

She was a force, too, and she's left a disaster in her wake.

The tunnel narrows and then curves sharply, opening into a domed room lined with all the workout gear a talent could ask for: targets of varying sizes for bullseyes, weights in the form of boulders and old machinery for strongarms, a laser grid that can be activated for wingtips, and, finally, a ring of perimeter crystal columns that can create a protective shield for bombshells.

The room is empty but for a single person in a vertical split, bending forward to touch the toes of her left foot, shorn head resting against her knee.

"Morning," I call, pitching my voice low in the echoing chamber.

Amethyst tips her head toward me and nods in acknowledgment. Her brown skin already shines with a layer of sweat.

I peel my windbreaker off and drop my backpack on one of the benches lining the wall, then join her in the middle of the cavernous room and stretch in a less impressive way.

"All good?" she asks, switching the direction of her split.

"Mm," I say.

"Cool," she answers.

This is what I like about Amethyst. She doesn't waste words, and she both appreciates and understands limited verbal communication.

No one will ever accuse either one of us of oversharing.

I used to spar with Ms. Jones, but after she all but collapsed the great hall—and if Tru hadn't literally thrown herself on top of Ms. Jones, the damage would have been a lot worse—I lost my sparring partner as well as my mentor. Who would want to train with a bombshell like me?

Amethyst. That's who. I'd only ever thought of her as one of Sage's friends, but after everything, she approached me.

"I want to join Underhill," she'd said. "But I need to make sure I'm good enough, and I can't think of a better way to do that than by training with a bombshell."

And when I asked her what I was going to get out of the

deal, she'd cracked one of her rare smiles and answered, "A partner."

It was so simple and so right. I don't know if most people make friends through negotiation, but it worked for us.

We stretch in silence, wrap our hands, then step into the ring of crystals. Amethyst hits the controls and there's a hum of energy as the translucent dome arcs above us. It's not strictly necessary—it only protects people outside the ring, and Amethyst is in it with me—but Underhill policy is very clear on this point: Any bombshell training within these tunnels must be done with a mentor present or within the confines of crystal columns like these.

I know from experience that waiting for Amethyst to attack is a fool's errand, so I don't. I dart forward, fists raised in a protective position. She steps to the left, faster than I can see, but not yet at her full speed. I swivel, aiming for where I think she'll be in another second and jab.

I miss, my knuckles catching only the wind of her passing as she circles around behind me. I know what's coming so I duck just in time to feel her jab sweep the air where my head was a second ago.

I don't have any hope of dodging the next, though, and can only brace for the blow that lands in my side.

I fall to one knee and roll, letting the momentum carry me a safe distance away so I'm ready for her next attack.

When we first started working together, I was worried that she would let the fact that I am a full year older than her—not to mention the daughter of an infamous bombshell—make her pull her punches. But Amethyst Sharp doesn't let much intimidate her.

She rushes me and I feint left, aiming my strike just ahead of her position.

Amethyst grunts, the blow landing against her shoulder.

"I guess we're warmed up," she says, dancing away with a smile in her voice. "Wanna start for real this time?"

"If you insist," I answer, shaking out my hands and resettling my stance.

She blurs at her full speed, and I counter her attacks by feinting and blocking, always doing my best to hold the center of the ring. The thing about fighting a wingtip is that they're fast, much faster than I have any hope of being, but their speed comes at the cost of their accuracy. Sometimes the best thing you can do is move slower than they expect. But if they get you on the run, you're dead.

I move as little as possible, forcing Amethyst to slow down enough that I land a solid blow to her chin and another to her chest. She grunts and laughs, and then hurtles her shoulder into my stomach, knocking me over.

"C'mon, Lila. I thought you wanted to spar," Amethyst taunts. "Stop holding back."

"You're the only person who says that to me, you know," I counter, rolling onto my knees. It's true, and it's also a much bigger ask than I think she realizes. As soon as I have my feet back under me, she's on me, driving me back with a flurry of jabs that come too fast for me to see.

My breath comes quick, my heart rate spiking under the

onslaught. She doesn't let up. Her attacks are at lightning speed, each blow stronger than the last until she's backed me up against the shield. I feel the hum as my shoulders press into the invisible dome, feel the crackle of energy there.

She doesn't relent. And she won't. Not until I tap out in defeat.

A few weeks ago, I might have.

My father taught me to practice staying calm to keep my talents under control. Ms. Jones taught me to practice taking hold of my talent with all my strength and bending it to my will.

In the ring with Amethyst, I shield my face and imagine a swell of water inside me, bracing against the sudden rush of that feeling, the water surging from my toes, racing up and up and up for the surface.

I have spent my life afraid of this feeling. Convinced that my grip on it was tenuous, so unstable that even attempting to use my talent was irresponsible. Believing that if I am not careful every second of every day, this feeling will overwhelm me, drag me along as though I am little more than a seashell caught in an undertow. I reach for it now, letting it build and grow on its own until the momentum of its tide feels like something I can mold and direct.

Most people think that there is a fire inside of every bombshell.

But there is no fire inside of me.

There is a song.

My skin heats, my breath quickens, and as I draw energy

into my core, a rhythm builds in my head, a bass beat that thumps in time with my pulse. Amethyst hasn't let up. She rains down blow after blow as the song grows louder in my mind, the beat joined by a sweeping melody that rises like the tide.

The song resonates in my skin. It makes me feel electric and weightless and so very alive.

And then I attack.

I move faster than before, my attacks narrowing to a single focus. Amethyst is still faster than me, but I see her as clearly as I see anything else. I can follow every step she takes. I can see where she will attack next, and I can sidestep, defend, attack first.

I step into the fight as it if is a dance. The song in my head grows louder and faster, speeding up to match the tempo of my punches, tempting me to give myself over to it completely. To let everything inside me expand and explode. To give myself a moment of that perfect, sweet oblivion.

I am tempted. I cannot ignore how much I want it, nor how easy it would be to let the song itself take control and sweep me away.

But I don't trust easy things.

I hold my tempo steady, the effort of maintaining control taking nearly all my strength. I match every move I make to the rhythm inside me until I know that I am directing the song and not the other way around.

This is as far as I usually go. Any further, and my grip

loosens, the beat runs away with me, building and building until I become nothing more than resonance and I explode.

I have purposefully done it twice in my life. Once, under the careful supervision of Ms. Jones, and once with Tru, whom I cannot hurt.

Both times, the moment I lost my hold on the beat of the song I became nothing more than a spear of panic evaporating inside a resonant energy strong enough to tear down walls. It's not an experience I'm eager to repeat, but the only way to learn how to control it is to try.

And that's why we're doing this.

I focus on moving in concert with Amethyst as if she is my partner in this dance. Then, carefully, I loosen the choke hold I have over the song.

And everything else slows down.

The hum in my head grows louder, the rhythmic bass beat dimming beneath it as heat floods through me and I slow to a standstill. Amethyst slows as well, stepping back to observe.

"You good?" she asks, calm despite her heavy breathing.

Sweat drips from my forehead and down my neck, but my skin is so hot that it doesn't last long before it evaporates. I grit my teeth and answer, "Good."

"You've got this," she says.

I nod, but it's all I can do to control my breath. The song drives through me, and the urge to let it race ahead is almost too strong to resist. I pull back on it, and it feels like I'm trying to stop a car by yanking on the back bumper. Any second, it's going to buck and drive forward with me in tow. I'm going to explode the way Ms. Jones did. The way my father did. The way bombshells always do.

Panic lances through me.

"Get out," I whisper. "Now."

Amethyst doesn't waste time. She has the protective ring deactivated and reactivated—with her safely outside—with speed only a wingtip can manage.

"Try your numbers," she says, voice firm and practical.

I nod and start a basic arithmetic sequence starting with one and adding three to each subsequent number: one, four, seven, ten. The rhythm of it requires just enough focus that it calms everything else, including the song.

I count until the numbers cross two hundred and I can breathe normally again.

"There you go." Amethyst's voice is gentle and approving. "Good work."

Exhaustion trembles through me, but the song has subsided, once again under my control.

"Doesn't feel very good," I say, closing my eyes and drawing in a deep breath. I feel fuzzy and cold, as though I'm teetering on the edge of a vicious sleep. "That was no better than last time."

"It also wasn't worse," Amethyst is quick to point out. "Come get some water."

I hear the barely audible hiss of the protective dome coming down, and when I open my eyes, I see that we've gained an audience. There are half a dozen Underhill Apprentices gathered just inside the door. None of them has ventured more than a few steps into the room, and it's clear from their expressions that they're afraid.

"Arrogant asses," Amethyst mutters, and then to them, she shouts, "We have the room for another ten!"

I hear a quiet chorus of "tick, tick, boom," as our audience retreats into the hallway, watching me as if any second I will lose control.

"Ignore them," Amethyst says, striding across the room to slam the door behind them. "If they had a single brain cell between them, they might realize that taunting a supposedly unstable person is a bad idea."

"Ignore them," I say.

"My own words?" Amethyst says, brows shooting up as she looks down her nose at me. "See, this is what people don't know about you, Lila Morgan. They think you're rigid and cold, but really you're funny," she deadpans.

"Hilarious," I return, matching her delivery.

"I bet if people knew how funny you are, you'd have more friends," she counters.

"Thanks for the warning," I say, pulling my windbreaker on and reaching for the water bottle in my bag.

We take our time leaving the room and step into a nearly empty hall. Most of the gawkers have made themselves impressively scarce, but one remains. He stands with his back against the opposite wall, legs crossed lightly at the ankle, and near enough that I meet his eyes. He has blond hair glazed blue by the lights in the hallway, and he watches me with what I can only call an amused grin.

Amethyst keeps her shoulder against mine as we pass.

"Do you recognize him?" I ask when we're a short distance away.

"No," she says. "But he looks like he knows you."

She's not wrong, but I'm absolutely sure that I've never met him. He looks a few years older than me, with knotwork tattoos wrapped around each forearm. Combined with the sharp cut of his jaw and his direct gaze, he would have left an impression.

"You want me to stick around?" she asks, cautious in a way that avoids being protective or overbearing. "We could go grab breakfast upstairs."

"I'm good." I give her a reassuring nod. When I look back to where the guy was standing, he's gone. "And I have a meeting with the boss today," I add, ignoring the sudden knot in my stomach.

"Right, your suspension," she says.

For two months, I haven't been allowed to work in the Office of Operations. For the first few weeks, it was because I was under investigation due to my proximity to Ms. Jones. Even after I was cleared of any "intentional wrongdoing," my suspension remained. But today, that suspension will end and I will finally be able to get back to work and my regular paycheck.

Amethyst continues, "I should have brought you a celebratory, um, protein drink or something. Coffee? A key to symbolize your metaphorical release from metaphorical bondage?"

I almost smile. "I'm not fancy. A protein drink would be perfect. But not until it's official."

"Next time, then," she says. "Do you have anything planned to celebrate?"

This time, I do smile. It's impossible not to when I think of Tru—her mosaic gray-brown eyes like winter storm clouds, the flush of coral in her pale cheeks, the way her hair is always doing its best to escape whatever ponytail or braid she's wrangled it into. She took me by surprise and makes every day just a little better than it would otherwise be.

"I do," I admit, though I can see by the knowing smile on Amethyst's face that she's guessed the answer. I say it anyway: "I have a date."

Boss Acosta's office isn't so much an office as it is a receiving room. The doors are open when I arrive and Boss Acosta, dressed in black slacks and a blouse of Executive gold, stands behind her desk with her head tipped down and her attention locked on a tablet. She's slight and lithe. She's also one of the most accomplished strongarms in the talented world.

Even though my mentor tried to murder her, she's been nothing but kind to me throughout my suspension, encouraging me to be patient and even offering me a loan to get me and Sage through two months without my usual paycheck. I turned it down, and Sage put her planning skills to work creating a budget that would get us through on ramen noodles and peanut butter.

I'm looking forward to telling her that we can buy a real vegetable again.

The second I reach the threshold, Boss Acosta's head snaps up, sharp eyes landing on me. She's striking: high cheekbones, dark eyes, and smooth brown skin that's slightly lighter in tone than her son's. One of Sage's friends and now, by default, mine, Embry Acosta inherited his looks from his mother, and arguably her intellect, too. But where she is the leader of Underhill, he goes out of his way to have as little to do with the organization as possible. It seems like a self-defeating way to rebel, but I guess his options are limited.

"Lila. Good morning." Boss Acosta raises a hand to wave me inside the room, and I note that she does not smile as she usually does to put people at ease.

"Good morning," I echo. She doesn't invite me to sit, so I stand, clasping my hands behind my back.

She doesn't speak, fixing me with an expression I can't decipher, but that leaves me feeling uneasy.

"I'm here about my—"

"I know," she interrupts, not unkindly. "You're here about your suspension."

She doesn't elaborate and when the silence stretches on too long, I start again.

"It's been two months," I say.

Again, she nods. "I know. Lila, please have a seat. There's something we need to discuss."

"Discuss?" I ask, that uneasy feeling whipping into nausea as I take one of the two chairs on this side of the desk.

She nods again, sitting to face me. "I'm afraid there's been a delay in processing," she begins, a barely noticeable pause preceding the word "delay" that tells me she's editing the truth. "And I can't lift your suspension just yet."

The anger that flares to life inside of me is familiar, so much my constant companion that I have no trouble throttling it before it can reveal itself on my face. There are questions I could ask, demands I could make, and a large part of me would like to shout that this isn't fair, but I'm certain fairness has nothing to do with this. This is politics.

The council that convened to charge Ms. Jones with treason was the same council that slapped me with a two-month suspension in the first place. Several council members argued for a much longer sentence despite clearing me of wrongdoing. I have no trouble believing that they've come up with some reason to justify prolonging my suspension. All I can do is continue to demonstrate that I am worthy of their trust. Shouting about fairness would do the opposite.

I clear my throat and ask, "How much longer?"

"Another month," she says.

I clamp my jaw tight and hope she doesn't see the way every muscle in my body goes rigid with anger.

"It's okay to be upset, Lila," Boss Acosta says. And I know she means it with kindness, but that's the whole point, isn't it? I am not allowed to be upset by this. By anything.

She continues, saying, "I know this isn't what we agreed to, and I apologize for that. People may think that I control everything that happens inside of these tunnels, but that's rarely true.

"I know you understand how delicate this situation is, and how important it is that we get it right. That means not rushing things. I'm certain that at the end of one more month, we can put this firmly behind us and you'll be fully restored to the Office of Operations. Okay?"

I do a quick calculation of the money in my bank account. One more month is possible, but only if I can get Sage to agree to a one hundred percent peanut butter diet.

"Sure," I say lightly. "One more month. Should I set up another appointment with your admin?"

Boss Acosta tips her head toward me. "Yes, but first, Lila, there's one more thing I wanted to discuss with you."

My heart sinks like a stone, but I force a polite smile. "What is it?"

"I know you've been taking bounties—" Unable to stop myself this time, I sit up straighter, mouth opening to argue, but she throws her hand up to stop me. "I'm not going to tell you to stop," she assures me. "You're still a sanctioned bounty hunter. But what I am going to ask you to do is to keep a much lower profile."

I shake my head, not understanding. "I thought I *was* keeping a low profile. I haven't used my talent in two months. Every bounty I've claimed has been through other means."

"I know, I know," she says, bobbing her head. "But you've been working with Tru and she is very visible right now. Intentionally so, but that kind of visibility, while good for her, isn't what you need right now."

"She's my girlfriend," I say, shock making my words soft and slow.

"I understand that, and I'm not saying you can't spend time with her, but I think it would be a good idea if you worked bounties apart from her until your suspension is up."

An image of Tru fills my mind—the way she lit up when I asked her to join me on our first joint bounty.

"It's just for another month," Boss Acosta continues. "Keep your head down and this will all blow over."

"I—" An argument is on the tip of my tongue, but I pull it back at the last second. Bombshells don't get to be upset. We don't get to be angry. Especially not when there are so many people waiting for me to show them just how quickly I can lose my temper. Which I suppose is Boss Acosta's point. I swallow hard and nod. "Okay," I agree.

Boss Acosta's smile softens beneath sad eyes. She starts to say something else, but her administrative assistant speaks up from the doorway behind me.

"Sorry to interrupt," she says, not sounding too sorry. "But your next appointment has arrived."

Boss Acosta's entire demeanor shifts. Her smile transforms from an almost maternal expression to an armored shield. She stands, smoothing her hands over her slacks to ease the wrinkled fabric, and snaps the cover of her tablet shut.

It's so sudden and swift that my curiosity is piqued.

"If you have any other questions or concerns, please feel free to make another appointment," Boss Acosta says, sweeping one arm out to catch my shoulders as she rounds the desk. "I'm afraid I'm out of time this morning."

She guides me to the door, where we're met by a group of at least a dozen people, most of them looking official in Executive gold or Operations blue. There's even a person dressed in Enforcer black, but I don't recognize them.

At the center of the entourage is a man who looks familiar, though I can't place him. Tall and white with silver hair, he walks with one hand tucked into the pocket of his pin-striped suit, the other resting casually over his middle, and casts his brown eyes across the room. A pale scar puckers one thick eyebrow, fixing an inquisitive air about him as though he is searching for something.

"Elena," he says in a baritone both commanding and weathered by age, and reaches for Boss Acosta's hand. "It has been some time."

It registers that he used her first name and not her title. I'm certain I've never heard that from anyone except Embry. But if it bothers Boss Acosta, she doesn't show it.

"Anderson," she says warmly, stepping forward to clasp his hand in hers. "It has, hasn't it? What brings you so far east?"

East. There is no organization like Underhill out west, but that doesn't mean there's no order. This man is Anderson Flynn, the storied and infamous Kingpin of the West. A ruthless, lawless man who gained power in all the worst ways.

The administrative assistant cups one hand at my elbow, indicating that I should keep moving toward the exit, and I don't resist. I would like to put as much distance between me and that man as possible.

But as the door closes behind me, I hear Anderson's answer and my stomach plummets: "I hear you have a bastion in your midst."

THE FIRST EXPLOSION OF LILA MORGAN

I was arguing with my father the day I officially became a bombshell.

We argued a lot. I wasn't afraid of him the way other people were. I was aware that he was dangerous—that other people watched him the way they watch storm clouds—but I had no reason to believe he was dangerous to me.

I don't even remember why I'd lost my temper anymore. It could have been about anything and nothing at all—maybe I wanted to go to a movie with my friends, maybe I was mean to my sister, maybe I was just angry about the world and needed someone to yell at. I was angry all the time back then. Perpetually anxious that something dark was lurking inside me, and once it made its way out, I would never be able to hide it again.

Whatever it was, my temper went from a low simmer to a full boil in a matter of seconds. So swift that even now I remember the propulsive force of it, like being caught in a riptide.

"You don't understand!" I shouted.

"Lila, I know it doesn't seem like it, but I do," he answered. "I may be the only person who does."

The idea of being anything like my father lit a fuse inside me.

"No," I said, throwing a hand up between us as my heart beat fiercely in my chest. "I'm not like you. I'm not like you. I will not be like you!"

The words tumbled as fast as my breath, leaving me lightheaded.

My father held up a hand, not to me, but to my mother or sister, warning them to stay out of the living room.

He saw what I was still trying to deny.

"Lila, I want you to hold on to the sound of my voice," he said with enough authority that I did exactly that. "I'm not going anywhere. Just keep breathing and this will pass."

There were notes in my mind—a strange, discordant music that tore at my thoughts, the beat of it fighting my efforts to do as he said.

I started to shiver; my body trembled against the sudden changes inside me. Tears streamed down my cheeks, and I felt like I was on fire. Like I was about to burn.

"Dad," I whimpered, afraid now.

The noise in my head was suddenly a catastrophic storm. I felt my edges fraying, my vision fading as a brilliant heat drilled into my skin.

The last thing I saw was my father. He closed the distance between us and swept me into his arms. There was a final, devastating beat and that was the last thing I knew.

The path to Tru's front door is littered with weeds and broken stepping-stones. I would say that it's obvious no real adults live here, except it's been this way since the first time I dropped Sage off at the curb, two years before Tru's adoptive father died. Logan Dire was very much a real adult, but Tru says he liked it this way. It helped them keep a low profile—they were neither the nicest house on the block nor the least nice. Now she weeds just enough to maintain that middling neighborhood status. And she's nailing it.

Dodging tufts of crabgrass and a bunny statue that was added by Sage, I reach the front door and pause. On a normal, non-date day, this is when I would enter my code and walk straight through the door as though I live here. Because, as hard as it is to believe, I do.

My suspension lined up perfectly with the end of my

lease. Since I'd already burned my safe house, not to mention the money it had taken to maintain it, that left me with no way to prove that I had enough income to remain a viable tenant, and the apartment complex refused to renew my lease. I lost my mentor, my job, and my apartment all in the space of a few days. Sage says that I'm operating under a "luck deficit," which is true even if it's magical-thinking nonsense.

Since Sage usually spends the summers with me instead of in the St. Isidor's dorm, it was too late to find a bed for her there, leaving us essentially homeless.

And then there was Tru. Without batting an eye, she suggested that we move in with her and wouldn't even consider taking rent, claiming that the mortgage was paid for and Logan left behind more than enough for her to cover the property taxes for at least the next five years.

So now I live with the girl that I'm also trying to date. Not to mention my little sister.

It's like we skipped all the awkward parts of getting to know each other and went straight to all the awkward parts of sharing things like a refrigerator or a washing machine or daily schedules.

Sage, being Sage, suggested that we create a set of rules to ease the tension.

"You know how they say 'good fences make good neighbors'?" she'd asked after calling a house meeting on our first night here. "Well, think of it like that. Good rules make good roommates. We'll call them 'A Guide to Cohabitating with Your Paramour.'"

"Sage," Tru said, blushing hard and avoiding my eyes.

"What? Am I wrong? I don't think I'm wrong," Sage continued, unapologetic.

I can't deny that Tru is especially cute when she's flustered, so I urged my sister on. "What are the rules?"

"I'm so glad you asked," she said, beaming. "Rule number one: All house expenses and chores must be shared equally. Rule number two: Dates must take place outside of the home. And rule number three: Absolutely *no* kissing (et cetera) inside the house."

I think Tru actually choked at the last one, but I was secretly glad Sage had said it all out loud. She saved us from having to negotiate similar terms for ourselves. Always count on Sage to see a need for a plan and put one in place.

Except now we're discovering the exceptionally awkward parts of planning a date while also knowing when one of us is taking a shower. With a steadying breath, I press the doorbell and tuck a bouquet of early summer flowers behind my back. The chime echoes softly through the house, and I turn my face to the hidden sec system camera that will announce my arrival to anyone inside.

I hear a tumble of footsteps, a dramatic pause, and then the door opens.

"Good evening, young miss," Sage says with a devilish smile on her angelic face. "Can I help you?"

"Sage," I say, a gentle warning in my tone.

"Yes, Lila?" she retorts, eyebrows raised expectantly.

In Logan's absence, Sage has taken it upon herself to play the role of overbearing protector in Tru's life. Whether Tru knows it or not. And I know from experience that the quickest way to get rid of Sage is to play along.

"Okay," I say, shifting on my feet. "I'm here to pick up Tru for a date."

"Oh, is that so?" she says, crossing her arms over her chest. "Does Tru know about this?"

"Sage, you know she does," I answer. "Just tell her I'm here, please."

"Hang on, I need a little more information about this 'date.'" She emphasizes the word with air quotes. "Where are you going and for how long?"

"We're going out to dinner, and we'll be back by ten because Tru has a pastry run in the morning," I say with the kind of strained patience that is reserved for irritating little sisters.

"Mm-hmm," she hums. "Where is this supposed restaurant located? And what kind of food do they serve? And what's that behind your back?"

"Why don't you come here and find out?" I say, taking a small step forward.

With a laugh, Sage jumps back and shouts at the top of her lungs, "Tru! There's someone here for you!"

"Why do you have to be this way?" I ask when the house stops reverberating.

Sage grins and gestures for me to come in. At the motion, my eyes catch on the old scars that wind around her fingers like vines of ivy, alternately pale and still glossy pink. Sage says, "Would you care to have a seat while you wait?"

"I'm here." Tru's voice precedes her down the stairs, and I stop at the sight of her.

The only time I've seen Tru Stallard fancy was the time she let my sister dress her for the Underhill Gala, and even then she stuck with a sensible shoe. Now she descends in a pair of fitted black jeans and matching top layered under a thin gray cardigan with two overly large buttons on the front. Her hair is up in one of her classic ponytails, but she wears no jewelry, no makeup.

And I have never considered myself to be the romantic type, but seeing her like this always leaves me breathless.

Sage likes to remind me that I had literal years to notice Tru before the night I shot her in the leg, and she's probably right. I knew of Tru the way I knew everyone who tried to get close to Sage: by name and reputation. In my book, Tru was more of a potential enemy than a potential friend.

I had good reason. In the wake of our father's death, people we'd considered friends turned out to be the opposite. Sage's supposed friends, in an effort to prove to the world that I was just like our father, tortured her, holding her hand in an open flame just to see if it would push me over the edge.

That's what I thought of the first time I saw Tru: the harm she could do to my sister.

The first time I *really* saw Tru, she was running for her life. Putting everything at risk for the sake of baby Thea, who she hardly knew. She was selfless and scared and, in the face of everything, doing the right thing.

She defies expectations and I love that about her.

"You look amazing," I say as she reaches the main landing.

Her eyes crinkle when she smiles, but only when she's caught off guard. Like now.

"I look the same as I always do," she says, tucking a stray curl behind her ear.

"That's what I said," I answer, pulling the flowers from behind my back. "No lavender," I say.

"I'll be the judge of that," Sage announces, snatching the bouquet from my hand.

"Sage Anastasia Morgan, give those back," I snap.

"I still can't believe that's your middle name," Tru says, reaching for the flowers and bringing them to her nose. "They're perfect."

"And I can't believe you don't *have* a middle name," Sage answers. "I mean, I guess you could use Grey now if you wanted. Gertrude Grey Stallard. It works."

"I'll consider it," Tru says, placatingly. "Ready?"

"Ready," I confirm.

"Okay, but remember, you promised to have her home by ten p.m. Any later than that, and I'm sending out the guard. Don't test me!" Sage follows us all the way to the door.

"We wouldn't dream of it," Tru promises, then under her breath she adds, "She doesn't really have a guard, does she?"

I consider it and offer the best answer I can: "Let's not find out."

Even though Tru and I have been dating for the past two months, this is our first official date. It turns out that it's difficult to find a time for a date when everyone involved is dealing with life-altering events including but not limited to a two-month suspension of all reliable funds that are necessary for things like taking a girl out to eat.

I picked a Mexican restaurant on Southwest Boulevard because Sage was merciful and let me know that Tru loves a Sonoran taco. The crowd is light when we arrive, partly because we picked Wednesday night and maybe mostly because there are no games tonight. My instincts kick in and I mark the two men at the bar—one older and Black with a beer bottle in hand and his eyes glued to the television screen hanging above the bar, the other white with a shock of blue hair and watching the door as though he's waiting for someone.

I turn back to Tru and find that she's doing the exact same thing—cataloging the room for potential threats and points of ingress and egress. She meets my eyes and we share a private grin.

She steps in to speak against my ear, pushing up on her tiptoes so that her cheek brushes mine, and a delicious shiver wends down my spine. "Blue hair is on the suspicious list," she says, and I nod in agreement.

We're seated in a corner of the room, and the server brings a basket of chips and two dishes of salsa to the table along with glasses of water and menus. It isn't what anyone would call expensive, but all I can see are the prices and how hard they'll hit my suffering bank account. And even though I've planned for this, the reality of another month with no paycheck looms over my shoulder, reminding me that everything I spend tonight is money I won't have tomorrow.

I need another bounty, but at the moment the only bounties I can claim are open calls. No one wants to hire a bombshell for a long-term job. My inbox is full of passes and rejections, and I could tell myself it wasn't really a problem when I thought I'd be reporting to Ops tomorrow morning. But now—

"I have to admit something," Tru says, cutting into my spiraling thoughts.

I raise my eyes to hers, waiting for the confession.

"I've never been on a date before," she finishes. A small flush climbs into her cheeks, staining them the perfect shade of pink.

I smile, something Sage says I should do more often, and say, "Me either."

Tru's eyes widen in sheer surprise. "Never? But you—you're so—"

"So what?" I ask.

"Well." She flushes again before answering. "Gorgeous."

I'm honestly not sure what to say to that, so I just smile at her. And it should be awkward, but she smiles, too, laughs, and all the tension that's been building between us tumbles over into something that's still awkward, but in a shared way.

"I think we'll figure it out," I say. "I'm pretty sure that right now we're just supposed to talk and eat."

"Right," Tru says, bobbing her head. "Oh! I should have asked already, but how was your meeting with Boss Acosta?"

My stomach pitches and twists with stress and frustration, but I keep it inside, where it belongs. I don't want Tru worrying about me. I'll tell them all eventually, but tonight is supposed to be fun. "It was fine," I say, and then I recall something. "Have you ever heard of Anderson Flynn?"

Tru frowns in thought. "It sounds familiar, but I don't think so."

"He's maybe better known as the Kingpin of the West—sort of Boss Acosta's less ethical counterpart."

"I *have* heard of him." She scrunches her nose in thought, digging up whatever information is buried in her memory. "The kids at school used to talk about how dangerous it is for talented folk out west because he's so powerful. There's nothing like Underhill out there, right?"

"Just him," I say. "And his personal and extensive army."

I hadn't heard much about him before joining Underhill either, but in my limited time as an Associate, I've heard more about Anderson Flynn than any other talent. He's brutal and ruthless, with as much power and influence as Boss Acosta but without the rules and regulations to constrain him. It's alarming enough that he's here, but the fact that he's sniffing around for Tru is even worse.

"Why do you ask?" Tru pops a chip loaded with salsa into her mouth and crunches down.

"I—" I don't want to alarm her or ruin our date with potentially sinister news that I can just as easily deliver tomorrow, so

I only say, "He had a meeting with Boss Acosta this morning."

"You saw him?" Tru leans forward.

I nod.

"I wonder what he wants," she muses, opening the door for me to tell her what little I know.

Thankfully, our waiter chooses that moment to come take our orders. The distraction lasts just long enough that by the time he leaves, we're onto the next topic of conversation.

Our food has just arrived when our phones buzz in unison, the telltale chime of BountyApp announcing a new bounty in our vicinity. The screens light up with the notification—a red badge hovering over the gold icon.

For a second, we both freeze, forks poised over steaming dishes. But the temptation is there.

"Should we . . ." Tru starts.

I hesitate because this is a date. But curiosity is like an itch.

"It can't hurt to look," I say. Tru has her phone in hand before I've finished my sentence, swiping to the app with expert speed.

I swing my chair around to her side of the table, leaning in to share her screen.

"It's a find bounty," she says, opening the post.

FIND BOUNTY: *SHIN SPLINTS*

To be returned to Underhill for questioning regarding a private matter.

REWARD: *$10,000*

SPONSOR: *Mercutio*

There's a picture attached of a man with a shock of blue hair and white skin. Our eyes meet, both of us picturing the man we'd spotted earlier at the bar. Tru is smiling. Beaming with the joyful anticipation she always gets before setting out to claim a bounty. It makes her entire face light up.

"I know this is a date, but . . . shall we?" she asks, effervescent.

Boss Acosta's warning rings in my head. This is exactly what she asked me to stop doing. But turning Tru down right now will change the entire night. It will become about me instead of us, and I may not be an expert on dating, but I'm pretty sure you're supposed to do things that are fun. Things that make each other happy. And the way Tru is smiling at me right now . . .

I nod as I drop enough cash on the table to cover our completely untouched meal. If we can claim this bounty, it will hardly matter. Even splitting it down the middle, I'll have enough to cover me for another month. That alone makes it worth the risk.

Besides, this bounty is essentially gift wrapped for us. There's never been an easier way to keep a low profile.

"Let's go," I say.

Shin Splints, a.k.a. the man with the blue hair, is still at the bar with his eyes on the door, assuming the threat has yet to arrive and not that it's already here. He holds a salt-rimmed margarita in one hand, but even from ten feet away, I can see that the ice is well into its glacial melt and he hasn't had a sip.

Of the five main categories of bounties—find, guard, capture, traitor, or kill—find bounties are the most varied. They can be as simple as tracking down a lost pet or item, or as complex as tracking down a person who doesn't want to be found. Sometimes the bounty specifies that it's "location only," which means once you've laid eyes on the person, you can record and report their location and that's that. Those are easier because there's no need to let the person know you were ever on their trail. But this is a "find and retrieve" bounty, which means in order to claim the reward, we'll have to take the target into Underhill.

It also means that this has been sanctioned by Underhill. The sponsor, Mercutio in this case, has brought their case—and their money—to Underhill and it's been approved, so whatever Shin Splints did, it's serious enough that Underhill has determined he has to show up to account for his actions.

"Why do you think he chose 'Shin Splints'?" Tru whispers.

As far as monikers go, I've heard worse, but I'm also terrible at guessing why people pick the names they do. Maybe he's bad at running? Which would be good for us since neither of us is a wingtip. The less he resists, the more likely we can do this without drawing any attention. But it could also mean that he's very good at running, which would not be great for us.

That's the problem and purpose of monikers. They're meant to afford us a measure of anonymity within the BountyApp system, and for most people I think it works. But when you're a bombshell like me or a bastion like Tru, anonymity doesn't last long.

"We can ask him when we have him in custody," I answer, gesturing for her to go around from behind while I catch his attention more directly.

Tru learned a lot from her adopted father, but the one thing she lacks is experience. She tends to work on instinct and training more than anything else, which means in a situation like this, when we haven't had time to develop a working strategy, it makes sense to give her the tasks involving stealth. Or hand-to-hand combat.

Shin Splits has such a laser focus on the door that he actually startles when I step up to the bar next to him. I flash him an apologetic smile, tipping my head the way Sage does when she's flirting with someone, and utter a choppy little laugh.

"Didn't mean to scare you," I say as Tru steps up on his other side, so softly that I'm positive he hasn't noticed her. But the bartender will, so we have to move fast.

"You didn't," he says, eyes snapping back on the door as it opens behind me. "I mean, you did, but it's not your fault. I'm just . . . looking for someone."

"Looking?" I ask, tipping my head down in a way that won't mean anything to him, but signals to Tru that it's time to move. "Or running?"

Alarm brightens his eyes, but it's too late. Tru has a hand around his wrist, his arm twisted up behind his back in a hold so effective he doesn't even try to fight it.

"Fuck," he whispers, but it's the note of defeat in his tone that gives me hope.

Now that I'm this close, I know he's barely older than me, which makes me wonder what he's done to be the subject of a find bounty worth ten grand.

Or if it's justified, a knowing voice whispers at the back of my mind.

"Have you settled your bill?" I ask.

He looks at me like I can't be serious, but I am. The server behind the bar doesn't deserve to lose a tip just because Tru and I want to claim a bounty.

"I—no," he admits.

"I've got it," says Tru, digging into her pocket for cash and tucking it beneath his still full glass.

"Great," I say. "You owe us twenty bucks. Let's go."

I hear Shin Splints grunt as Tru gives his arm a warning tug, and then we leave the restaurant, arm in arm, like three old friends.

"You don't have to hold my arm so tight," he says, grimacing as we cross the parking lot toward Tru's car. "I'm not going to run."

"We'd prefer not to take your word for it," I say, taking Tru's keys from her pocket and clicking the button to unlock the doors.

It's going so well, that I almost feel silly for my earlier concern. We'll turn him over and claim our reward, and we might still have time to find another restaurant and finish our date.

But no sooner has that thought crossed my mind than I see a figure crossing the parking lot, his eyes dead set on us.

Tru notes him as quickly as I do and slows her pace.

Shin Splints gives a humorless chuckle. "Looks like we have company."

I clock his distance to us and the car as well as the likelihood that he saw the flash of the car's headlights when it unlocked and knows exactly where we're headed. If he's anything but a wingtip, it's a draw, which isn't good enough.

As he gets closer, his features come into focus enough that I recognize his blond hair and knotwork tattoos binding each forearm from this morning.

And he's not watching us; he's watching *me*.

Without another thought, I press the button to pop the trunk and push the key fob into Tru's back pocket.

"I'll take care of this," I say. "Put him in the trunk and get him to Underhill."

"The trunk!" Shin Splints whines. "Oh, c'mon, I said I wouldn't run. Do you have any rope? You can tie me to the seat if it makes you feel better."

"No time," I say without apology.

"Do you know him?" Tru asks with a glance at the blond guy, pushing Shin Splints ahead of her.

I shake my head. "Not yet. I'll see you at home."

"Are you—"

"I'm sure," I say. "Collect the bounty and I'll meet you at the house."

Hoping that I'm right about this and he's not actually here for the bounty, I run away from Tru and the car, darting over the railroad tracks toward the shelter of sweeping overpasses. A glance back proves that I was right: He's on my tail and Tru is peeling out of the parking lot with our bounty safe inside the trunk.

My pursuer is fast enough that I can't outrun him, so I

stop in the lee of the overpass of I-35 and turn to face him. He hesitates and comes to a stop when he's still several feet away.

"You're Lila Morgan," he says. Not a question, so I don't bother answering.

"Who are you?" I ask.

He shrugs. "A friend. Probably."

"Probably? What is that supposed to mean?"

Instead of answering, he holds his hands out to his sides, fingers splayed wide. I hear a resonate hum singing a low and steady note, and before I can fully comprehend what's happening, his palms begin to glow with a pale, ethereal fire that can only mean one thing: He is a bombshell.

I adjust my stance just as he rushes me, darting forward with lightning speed, striking out. The blow lands against my shoulder with a *boom* that rumbles in the grit beneath our feet.

I throw up my hands and open my mouth to protest, but he's already rounding for another attack. This time I block, letting instinct guide me as he comes around again and again. He's insistent and aggressive. I hardly have time to regain my balance between blows before another is on its way, and each attack is accompanied by that loud boom.

It's the opposite of keeping a low profile, but he doesn't seem to care.

Sweat gathers at my temples and I continue to deflect, but instead of losing steam, he's gaining it.

He knocks me back and I slip, dropping one hand to the gritty asphalt to regain my balance. He's on me in that moment. One arm wrapped around my throat, the other pulling me tight against him, hauling me up so that he can speak into my ear.

"You fight like a . . . what's the word you use around here?" He pauses for effect before snapping his fingers. "Oh, right: topsider," he says, and I swear there's humor in his voice.

"I know," I grind out, shifting my grip on his solid forearm, then I throw my hips back and drive one elbow into his ribs. He was ready for it, but that doesn't always matter. He buckles, sidestepping just enough that I can swivel out of his hold.

I stagger forward, gasping for breath and doing my best to keep a sharp eye on him. But he just stands there. Watching me.

"Why are you following me?" I say between breaths.

He considers me for a moment before answering. "Because I thought you might have an edge."

"An edge?" I stand up straight, still breathing hard, still ready to fight.

"I thought you might be interested in being an actual bombshell. Not an Underhill puppet," he clarifies.

"I'm not a puppet," I say, not sure why I feel the need to defend myself to this person.

"You fight," he says, enunciating each word, "like a topsider." He runs a hand through his tousled blond hair and shrugs again as if none of this is his fault. He adds, "Underhill teaches you to be small. And you're letting them. Just like your dad."

The anger I work so hard to restrain surges to life, a thumping, hungry baseline beat that matches my pulse. It drives forward and I let it, channeling the rush of energy into my fists as I dive at him.

Delighted laughter greets me even as I land a blow to his jaw. I strike again, harder, funneling more energy through my body, into my muscles and knuckles until I can hardly feel them. I reverberate with the sound of this wild song; I am electric and limitless.

And all at once, I realize that I have gone too far.

The song is rushing through me, picking up speed and momentum, outstripping my ability to pull it back. It pulses and pounds. It wants to go, go, go and with each beat I feel my control slipping.

In another minute, I will explode and if there is anyone nearby, they will die.

Panic sharpens my mind. But only just. Only enough that I can see the guy who chased me out here and challenged me to this fight. He's not running. He's standing there, two feet from me. His eyes are clear blue, and he's not smiling anymore.

"Lila," he says, commanding what little attention I have left. "Don't be afraid of yourself. That's what Underhill wants. But fear makes a rotten foundation."

The power inside of me sings louder, reverberating through my bones and tissue until there is no difference between them. I know I still have a mouth—tongue, teeth, lips—but I can't remember how to use them . . .

"I . . . can't," I say, breathing hard. At least I think I am.

The guy nods. "You can. But not today. This is far enough."

He steps behind me, and this time when he wraps an arm around my neck and applies pressure, I don't resist. I close my eyes, and that's that.

Waking up is painful and disorienting. I'm not beneath an I-35 overpass, which is a good thing, but there's a whooshing sound that sounds like traffic.

I peel my eyes open to find that I'm lying on a bench inside Union Station as a train pulls away on the other side of the glass. It's dark outside, but the clock on the wall suggests I've only been unconscious for about an hour. And I'm alone. Or not alone—I count three other people inside the waiting room as I push myself up to sitting. One of them gives me a little wave before turning to leave. He's wearing long sleeves over his tattooed arms.

He knocked me out, brought me here, and then stuck around to make sure I was, what? Safe? Alive? Both? I think I should be irritated, but my head is pounding and I just want to get home. I can be irritated later.

I get to my feet and count to ten before I trust my balance

enough to try walking. I'm pretty sure the attendant behind the counter thinks I'm drunk or high or something equally unlikely.

I smooth my hair back and check that my phone and wallet are still in my pockets, and then I hold my head high and aim my steps for the front of the station.

"Lila!" My name echoes through the main hall and I turn, surprised to find Tru crossing toward me.

It takes me a little too long to realize that I shouldn't be surprised because Underhill is directly beneath us. Tru had to come here to claim the bounty.

"I'm sorry that took so long. I swear they change the process every single time," she says when she reaches me. Then she stops, eyes narrowing on what is probably a bruise on my cheek judging by the way it throbs. "Are you okay? Are you hurt? Did that guy hurt you?"

There is no easy answer to that question. There's a simple one, but not an easy one. I force a small smile. Just enough to case her concerns. "I think I made a friend," I say. "How about you? All's well?"

She laughs. "All's well. You know, sometimes you really remind me of Papa Logan. He used to say things like that. Like he was a knight in a fairy tale."

"Sounds like a compliment to me," I say.

"It is," she answers. The smile on her face softens the way it always does when she talks about Logan. Which isn't often.

Sage thinks we should encourage her to talk about him

more. She's concerned that Tru is in denial about his death because she won't talk about it, won't even go visit his grave. But given that her entire paradigm has shifted in the past two months, I think a little denial is understandable. She's dealing with a lot, and the fact that she mentions him at all is a win. "Did everything go okay for you?" I ask.

Tru grins triumphantly as we continue toward the entrance. "Apart from the delay downstairs, it was easy. Our bounty is in the bank and half will be winging its way to you shortly. I also found out why he's called Shin Splints." With a laugh, Tru explains how when she went to get him out of the trunk, he'd worked himself lose and was ready to fight. "Turns out, he's a bullseye and his favorite trick is beaming you in the shins with a marble."

"That sounds painful," I say. "For most people."

She laughs again. "He was *not* expecting to meet a bastion today, I can tell you that. I almost felt bad for him."

Old Mr. Bern is seated at the doors on the east side of the entrance politely nodding to the few people still coming and going at this hour. To any topsider, he's just a Union Station employee who dresses up in an old-fashioned conductor's uniform and greets folk as they come to visit. To us, he's an Underhill official who grants access to the elevators that take us down to the offices.

He used to be stationed next to the elevators at the end of the main hall, but they've upped security in the past two months and now he's out here.

"Looks like a successful evening, Miss Stallard," he says when we approach. "And, Miss Morgan, I didn't realize you were in." He peers down at his tablet in some confusion.

"I came in through the back entrance," I say, relieved to know that my handsome frenemy was not only considerate of my safety but also circumspect. "I got delayed and thought I'd just meet Tru up top, which I did."

"Ah, that explains it," he says with relief. "You had me worried for a second because you, Miss Morgan, are memorable. I always remember when you walk through my doors. Even when you were only so high." He holds his hand out to demonstrate, then snaps it in again. "Don't you listen to what they're saying, Miss Morgan. There are plenty of bad people in the world, plenty of bad actors as they say, but you have always been a cut above. Your actions speak for themselves."

He says it with a grandfatherly smile, and I know he means well, but it curdles in my stomach. Sour and thick.

"Thank you, Mr. Bern," I say, reaching out to grab Tru's hand. "Good night."

"Good night, Mr. Bern," Tru calls over her shoulder as I hurry us out into the dark parking lot.

The early summer night is warm, the air still thick, but I draw in a deep lungful and push it out again.

"You okay?" Tru asks, tugging my hand a little.

"I'm fine," I say. "Just beat, and not looking forward to the way Sage is going to grill us about tonight."

Tru sucks a breath in through her teeth. "She's going to be deeply disappointed in us," she muses.

"Deeply," I repeat, checking the time on my phone. "And we won't make it home by ten."

Tru stares into the distance for a second, obviously imagining all the ways Sage is going to express her dissatisfaction with our first date. Then she nods to herself and says, "Well, the only way out is through, right? Let's go."

I half expect Sage to be waiting at the front door when we pull up, arms crossed and a look of parental displeasure on her face. She's not. She's waiting just *inside* the door. Arms crossed, lips pursed, a phone held toward us with the time illuminated.

Tru holds up her hands like she's going to plead for mercy, but I stride straight past my little sister and into the kitchen, where I grab a plastic baggie and a dish towel and begin to make an ice pack for my still throbbing cheek.

"You promised to be home by ten p.m. I can't be the only responsible one around here. Do you know how much I worry about you? You do both remember that it was only a short time ago that we were all on the run from actual assassins, right?"

Sage is talking while she walks after me. Alternately directing her words at me and at Tru, sharing the love.

"We know," Tru says as soon as she's able to get a word in. "We're barely late, and we have a good reason."

"Okay, a good reason. What is—" She turns her full attention on me, finally noticing what I'm doing. "What's going on? What happened to your face?"

She stops, and for full drama, brings one hand to her chest. "Tru," she asks. "Did you two have a fight?"

Tru sort of gasp-laughs. "Are you asking me if I *hit* your sister?"

"We took a bounty, Sage!" I cut in. Nothing like ripping the Band-Aid off.

But the sting is evident.

All of Sage's previous bravado fades to nothing. It's as if she's a speaker and someone came by and turned the volume all the way down. She just sort of deflates.

"You took a bounty?" she asks. "But—without me? Another one?"

I think I will always marvel at my sister's ability to prioritize emotion. Two seconds ago, she was ready to rake us over the coals for missing our completely arbitrary curfew by five minutes, and now she's devastated.

It's a sore spot between us and has been since the first time Tru and I took a bounty without inviting Sage to join us. I didn't think anything of it at the time, but I should have. Just like I should have thought about her tonight.

"It was right there," I say, trying to soften my approach. "Did you see that find bounty? It was for someone *in* the restaurant with us and it was too good to pass up." I almost add that we need the money, but I really don't want to compound the tension of this moment with yet more tension.

"It wasn't even that exciting," Tru adds. "He barely put up a fight."

"Then what happened to your face?" Sage asks.

"I—" I start, but Tru intercedes.

"Another bounty hunter showed up and Lila distracted him while I claimed the bounty," she explains. Which is mostly true even if there's more to the story.

Sage gives this some thought, and I can see her trying to hold on to her anger and her hurt, but it doesn't take more than thirty seconds before her heart wins and she's at my side, clucking like a mother hen.

"Keep the ice pack on for about ten minutes or however long you can tolerate the cold. It will help keep the bruising down," she says as if I haven't done this dozens of times before. But I let her because I know it makes her feel better. It makes me feel better, too.

"Thanks. It's really not that bad," I promise her.

"Good," she says, and then she steps back, some of that fire from earlier returning. "Because I cannot believe you two failed your first date!"

"Failed seems harsh," Tru protests, but there's a flush in her cheeks. "We just had a change of plans."

"If that 'change of plans' involved doing things you do on a typical workday and frequently with your little sister slash best friend, then it wasn't a date." She crosses her arms defiantly. "You need a do-over. But not tonight. Tonight has been exciting enough. It's time for bed."

"Are you going to plan our next date?" Tru teases as Sage turns to go upstairs.

"Don't tempt me, Tru Stallard," Sage retorts, already halfway up the stairs.

I catch Tru's hand before she can follow, pulling her close. "She's not wrong," I say. "But we can still end the night in the right way."

Tru's eyelashes flutter and her lips flash into a quick smile, nervous and excited. Her eyes find my lips and I know she's thinking the same thing I am. "What about rule number three?" she whispers.

I flick my eyes toward the top of the stairs to make sure Sage isn't spying on us, then I tug Tru's hand. She follows me as I silence the sec system and we step out onto the front porch.

"We are technically not inside the house," I say, stepping down to the sidewalk and turning to face her.

One step up, she's the same height as me, her eyes level with mine. She bites her bottom lip, a sweet smile blooming beneath the pressure.

"We won't be breaking any rules," she whispers, and her breath is warm against my chin.

Without releasing her hand, I slide mine along her waist to the small of her back, tugging her against me so that we are locked together. I feel her tense. Then melt.

My breath is as hot as hers and I want nothing more than to kiss her, but I hover a whisper away, our lips brushing softly against one another. It is this—the nearness of her—that ignites a fire inside of me. Urgent and greedy until I can hardly stand it.

I drop my mouth to hers and we kiss.

She lets me take the lead. Lips parting at the slightest pressure. And then I don't really know who's leading and who's following, if there even is such a thing with kissing. I only know that I've been tossed on the ocean and every surge comes with a surrender, every caress with a shiver, and I want nothing more than to give myself over to the tides.

The Second Explosion of Lila Morgan

As a reward for surviving my first bombshell experience, my father took me on a father-daughter day trip to Middle of Nowhere, Missouri.

In some ways, I was lucky that my talent had arrived during the summer months, when I wasn't constantly in school and around my peers. But in others, it was the worst time in the world.

I was a new bombshell in need of experience, and the best place to practice being the human equivalent of a deadly weapon was anywhere people weren't. To my father, that meant a seemingly endless tallgrass prairie far from towns, roads, farms, and any other decent source of air-conditioning or shade.

"Dad, it's too hot," I complained as sweat trickled down my back to soak the waistband of my jeans, which I was only wearing to protect myself from ticks and snakes.

My father was seated in front of me, both of us cross-legged in a little crater of grass. His eyes were closed because we were supposed to be meditating. Listening for the sound of our talent, that's how he described it. Listening for it until it was all I could hear.

"How am I supposed to concentrate like this? I'm going to burn."

I meant a sunburn, but his eyes flicked open at my comment and snapped to mine.

"That's the point," he said. "You can't learn to control your talent if you never experience it."

"I don't *want* to experience it," I protested.

For a week after that night in the living room, I hardly spoke to anyone. It took me three days to agree to leave my room again, four to step outside the house. I didn't trust myself anymore—I didn't know how. Everything I knew was different, and I wasn't the only one who'd changed.

My father went from the distant, yet loving person he was my whole life to something almost the opposite. Always near and overbearing, all his attention suddenly on me.

"You don't have that choice," he snapped back. "You must know what it feels like so you can learn how to stop it."

"But I know what it feels like."

"No, you—"

"I don't want to do it again!" The memory was so fresh. My body shivered with echoes of it despite the heat.

My father looked at me sadly, as though he regretted nothing more than the fact that I was his daughter. For just a second, I thought he'd relent, he'd tell me we could try again later, we'd go home and maybe watch a movie with Mom and Sage. But I didn't know this version of my father. Not yet.

"You can choose when," he said, closing his eyes again. "But we'll stay here until you do it."

My anger flared and, with it, that haunting note that was forever buzzing in the back of my mind. Keying into it was like touching a live wire. The notes were an assault, reverberating so fiercely that I heard nothing but the surge of my blood, felt nothing but the heat of my heart, saw nothing but the fading summer sky as my vision went white.

I realized then that my father was right, I had not felt *that* before. I had felt a version of it, but a paler, more controlled version. One that stopped halfway to completion. I had not experienced the full and exhilarating euphoria of my bombshell talent that night in my living room.

I realized it in that moment, but never stopped to question what it meant.

Never stopped to wonder: Why not?

The summons arrives before my alarm. A message from Boss Acosta to come to her office ASAP. Not a request or a suggestion, an order.

I'm awake in an instant. If this is about last night, my morning is going to be rough.

I slip out of the bed I share with Sage, making just enough noise that her subconscious brain doesn't key into the fact that I'm sneaking out. Sage is notoriously difficult to wake, but ironically it happens more frequently when I try to be quiet. She can sleep through a storm but the sound of a faucet dripping down the hall will perk her right up.

I grab a change of clothes and my bag and double-check that she's still asleep before opening the door. She sleeps flat on her back, looking absurdly peaceful with her long blond hair in a loose braid and one leg always outside of the covers. The same way she's slept since we were little.

Sharing a room again has been as much of an adjustment as living with my girlfriend. I thought I would hate it, but I don't think it's possible to hate anything about Sage.

The bruise on my cheek makes brushing my teeth a treat. I consider whether I should try to hide it with concealer, but decide leaving it uncovered may be in my favor. My one and only defense is that I was facing off with a bombshell who was doing his best to *not* keep a low profile. Maybe seeing evidence of my fight will help convince her that I wasn't behaving recklessly.

I *was* taking a bounty, but even that isn't so cut and dry. Tru did most of the work on her own. I wasn't even there when she brought him to Underhill.

The sun has barely risen and the house smells deliciously of fresh baked goods, lemon and cinnamon and yeasty dough that makes my mouth water. By the time I make it downstairs, Tru is gone. She does this several times a week—waking well before dawn to bake round after round for delivery to half a dozen local coffee shops. It's an impressive operation.

She left a small plate of croissants out for the taking, but I grab a protein shake from the fridge and head out into the muggy morning air. In the interest of time, and of not dragging this out any longer than necessary, I skip my usual morning jog and drive the short distance to Union Station.

Mr. Bern is already seated just inside the glass doors, his conductor's hat perched over tufts of snow-white hair. He gives me a warm smile when I step inside.

"Good morning, Miss Morgan," he says, putting me at ease simply by being himself.

"Is the old station open for visitors?" I ask, giving him the code even though he knows who I am.

There are several ways in and out of the Underhill tunnels, but they aren't always open. Bern is the gatekeeper, checking us in and making sure we make our way to the correct doors at the correct times.

"Let me check," he answers before turning his attention to the tablet in his hand and tapping at the screen. "The museum entrance is open this morning. You're welcome to use it."

"Thank you," I say, and then, following his instructions, I head for the museum tucked into the corner of the main hall.

There's hardly ever anyone in the small gallery, but I double-check that I'm not being watched before stepping through the door at the back. At the end of a narrow corridor, there's another door but this one has no knob, no visible way to unlock it except with the small screen next to it on the wall. I wait for the light to flash green, my indication that Mr. Bern has given me temporary authorization, then press my thumb to the screen. It's a dynamic sort of two-step authentication process that gives me access to a private elevator. From here it only goes down.

The ride is fast, taking me through nearly a hundred feet of stone and earth to the caverns below. The old-fashioned dial above the doors swings to "B" and will stay there as I descend.

At the bottom, the elevator opens into a small chamber, the

walls round and smooth as if someone blew a bubble out of stone. A single tunnel dives into a river of electric-blue lighting. The blue lights here indicate that I'm in Operations; by the time I reach the Executive zone, they've turned sunny and gold.

Boss Acosta's door is open when I arrive, her administrative assistant posted just outside at her desk. She nods when she spots me and gestures at the door.

"Good," Boss Acosta snaps almost before I've entered the room. She points at the chair in front of her desk and adds, "Sit."

I strangle the urge to refuse on principle and do as I'm told. The doors click shut behind me and Boss Acosta folds her arms over her chest.

She gazes down at me, not in anger or irritation, not in puzzlement, but with unnerving detachment. It's in moments like these when I'm reminded, on an almost primal level, why she is the one in charge of Underhill, Inc.

"I assume you have an excuse for what happened last night, Lila, but I have to say, I'm not interested." She sits, folding her hands in front of her on the desk. "It doesn't matter what the reason was, we have ended up in the same place."

"What place?" I ask, swallowing the panic that pinches my throat.

"A place that is worse than it was yesterday." As she answers, she reaches for a tablet, swipes at the screen, then swivels the screen to face me.

It's a video, probably from a traffic camera, and there's

no mistaking what it's captured. Two figures, too small and indistinct to be easily recognized, stand beneath an overpass, trading blows until one begins to shimmer, hands glowing like twin stars.

Even though I know what's coming next, I can't look away. I see the moment we pause to argue and feel more than see the exact second he uses my father to goad me into activating my own talent. I begin to glow, not in the gradual way he did, but all of a sudden. The energy radiates and ripples dramatically as if a stone were dropped into a pool of water.

It ends the way I know it will, with my nameless friend choking me into unconsciousness. I go limp, but before I can reach the ground, he effortlessly lifts me in his arms and carries me out of frame.

I'm not prepared for how that makes me feel, so I'm almost relieved when Boss Acosta lets the tablet fall back onto her desk and levels me with an intense gaze.

I assume she's determined for herself that I didn't start the fight, and that she doesn't care. It happened and when it comes down to it, I used my talents in public.

"You might think that I have some sort of control over this situation," Boss Acosta says, breaking the tension. "But just because this video made its way to me doesn't mean I am the *only* person who has it. In fact, that almost guarantees I am not. Someone else out there now knows that you—hard as it may be to identify your face in this video—used your talent in a public place. That's not a good thing right now."

"Was it ever?" I say before I can think better of it.

Boss Acosta gives me a withering look, but she doesn't seem as bothered by my back talk as I might have expected. In fact, I think she might agree with me.

"People are on edge," she continues. "It's not your fault, but it is your burden to bear, as much as it's mine."

"And what about the guy who attacked me? The other bombshell?" I ask. "Are you going to call him in, too? Is it his burden to bear or only mine?"

Boss Acosta's expression shutters. "He's not your concern."

"Not my concern?" I repeat, not sure I heard her correctly. "There are only a handful of bombshells in Underhill. He isn't one of them."

"Not your concern," she says again. "If you see him again, don't engage."

I snap my mouth shut. He's gone out of his way to make himself my concern, but if she's going to insist otherwise, maybe I should be equally tight-lipped.

"Right," I say, drawing in a deep breath. "What else can I do for you today, boss?"

"I need you to hear me, Lila," she says. "If this gets out," she says, gesturing to the table, "things are going to get much worse. Not only for you, but for the people around you."

Sage is on the cusp of her senior year at St. Isidor's. She has her heart set on attending the gala, finding a mentor, and becoming an Underhill Apprentice.

None of that will happen if her reputation is tainted by being related to a bombshell who can't follow instructions. In addition to the one who killed twelve people all those years ago.

"Do you understand what I'm saying?" Boss Acosta asks.

She's saying that if I can't convince people that I'm not a threat the way my mentor was, the way my father was, then Sage won't have a chance at the future she wants.

And it will be my fault.

I nod. "I got it," I manage. "Is that all?"

Boss Acosta purses her lips, perhaps considering something to ease the humiliation of this moment. I'm glad when she decides against it. "That's all," she says.

I'm not sure I draw a full breath until I'm outside Union Station again.

The sun is up. Hot and glaring and quickly inspiring a layer of sweat. I walk without paying any attention to where I'm going. Straight ahead, across the street, into the grass, and up.

I'm too angry, too frustrated and shamed, and choking on the injustice of it all to do anything but keep moving, so it takes me a minute to realize that someone is calling my name.

"Lila!" he calls, that voice ingrained in my recent memory. "Lila Morgan, wait!"

As much as I hate to admit it, I have to consider the possibility that Sage is right. I am operating under a severe luck deficit. There's no other explanation for running into the person Boss Acosta just told me to avoid.

I pick up the pace, muscles warming as the ground slopes uphill. I can hear him start to jog behind me.

"Lila!" he tries again, closer this time. "I just want to talk."

I spin on my heel so abruptly that he nearly collides with me. His blue eyes flash in sudden alarm, and he takes a startled step back.

"Why are you here?" I snap. "Are you following me? Or were you just waiting to see if I'd come to Underhill today?"

"Yes," he answers.

I'm so surprised that it takes me a second to recall my question. "Yes, to which?"

"Well, both if I'm being honest, but this morning it's the latter."

"You were . . . waiting around just hoping to find me?"

He winces and runs a hand through his blond locks. "It seemed less intrusive than following you home last night or putting a trace on you."

I stare, not sure what is more concerning, the fact that he's stalking me or the fact that he's willing to come right out and say it.

"Who are you?" I ask.

A mischievous smile tips one corner of his mouth. "My name is Ryan. It's a pleasure to meet you." He extends a hand to me.

It's a ridiculous gesture considering all that's happened between us, but I take it and then I take a second to notice the things that didn't register when we were locked in active combat. He's maybe two inches taller than me, lithely muscled, and actually quite handsome. I also note that, like me, he took home a few souvenirs from our last encounter. An indigo bruise blooms around his left temple and there's a smaller, greener one at his chin.

I hope they both hurt.

"What do you want from me, Ryan?" I ask.

He considers for a moment, then his smile fades and he leans closer, nothing but the utmost sincerity in his blue eyes when he says, "I want to show you *what* I am."

I have a second to wonder what he means before his hand begins to heat in mine. His skin begins to glow ever so slightly. And then I hear it—a song that is so like my own, but different. Like a variation on a theme. I can feel it reaching out to me until it echoes in my mind and my own song begins to respond.

With a gasp, I yank my hand away. He doesn't try to stop me.

"What the hell?" I ask, stepping back so there's a few feet of distance between us.

"Interesting," he says, but he makes *interesting* sound like *pathetic*. "I thought you'd worked with other bombshells before."

"I—I have," I stammer, confused and also defensive. Aside from my father, I've worked with one other bombshell, but she, as it turns out, was far from reliable. "What does that have to do with anything?"

"Ah," he says in a way that makes me feel he understands more than I really want him to.

He glances around, drawing attention to the fact that we're standing on the side of the hill that leads up to Liberty Memorial. "Maybe you'd like to talk somewhere else?"

"After last night?" I ask. I think about telling him that Underhill says he's not worth my concern. It's not exactly the truth, but close enough. But then I remember his words from last night. *Underhill teaches you to be small. And you're letting them.*

He follows me as I resume my climb up the hill, undaunted by my rejection. "I don't mean to be patronizing, but I think I can help you."

I laugh. "What makes you think I need your help?"

"After last night?" he asks, humor simmering in his voice. "I don't think it. I know."

"I—" I hesitate. I want to tell him he doesn't *know* anything about me, but he clearly does. He knows my name, my talent, and my history. And he knows how to control his own talent.

Boss Acosta's warning rings in my ear. *If you see him again, don't engage.*

"Fine," I say. "Let's talk."

At the top of the hill, we find a space in the shadow of the World War I memorial and take a seat on the stone dais holding one of the two limestone sphinxes at its base. I know one of them is "Memory" and the other "Future," but I can never remember which is which. Both cover their eyes with massive wings.

"Okay. Let's back up to who you are," I say. "Why haven't I seen you in Underhill before yesterday?"

"Because I'm not local," he says. "I'm originally from Northern California, but I work in Vegas. You know Anderson Flynn?"

"Not personally," I say. I don't volunteer that I saw him entering Boss Acosta's office yesterday morning. "But I know he's in town."

"I work for him, but don't worry. I'm just security, along for the ride."

He must see the confusion on my face because he laughs and adds, "I know. Who hires a bombshell to be on their security team? I get that a lot."

"He must have a lot of trust in you," I say.

"More than Underhill has in you," he says as though he's commenting on the weather and not my entire life.

"You don't know anything about my relationship with Underhill," I bite back.

"Not the details," he admits. "But I know that they will pretend to trust you until the minute you do something they view as wrong, and then all bets are off. Just like I know that ever since Ms. Jones attacked the boss, you've been sidelined despite being more capable than half the talents in this city. Probably more than half."

"I haven't been sidelined," I protest, even though I know he's right.

He lets that go. "You have skill," he continues. "And if you continue trying to do what they expect of you, you'll pull a muscle, lose that control you're working so hard to gain, and fulfill that age-old bombshell prophecy and die young. You know how the vibration gets more intense the harder you try to hold on to it?"

I do, but I don't want to admit that to him.

It occurs to me that even though he's doing most of the talking, I still don't know nearly as much about him as he does about me.

"How do you have so much control?" I ask.

"I wouldn't call it that." He laughs a little, tousling his hair. "Control is what others want from us. Because it's something they can understand. You see a bomb lying on the ground, and you want to control it; prevent it from being ignited by shoving it into a protective container or defusing it. That's how Underhill treats people like us—like bombs constantly on the verge of obliteration."

"Aren't we?" I ask. "All talents require control, but it matters more for us. If we don't learn control, we explode. We kill people."

"We explode because we're constantly trying not to," he counters quickly. "We apply pressure to a system with no room for it, and it has to find an outlet someway. But that's other talents forcing us into a framework they understand when we need something they don't even have the context to understand."

"What do we need?" I ask.

He leans close enough to whisper, "Resonance."

The word hums along my skin, tickling the small hairs inside my ear and sinking all the way through me—a drop of water into an ocean.

"You'll never get what you're after if you keep playing by their rules," he says. "Ms. Jones wasn't right, but she also wasn't wrong. And I think on some level, you know that."

I want to argue, but a firm weight has settled on my chest and all I manage is a cold glare.

Reaching into his pocket, Ryan produces a small card and offers it to me.

"If you ever get tired of playing by their rules, give me a call," he says.

I pocket the card without looking at it. "Are you going to show me a whole new world?" I ask with mock wonder.

He grins, climbing back to his feet. "Just a new way of being in this one. But only if you want."

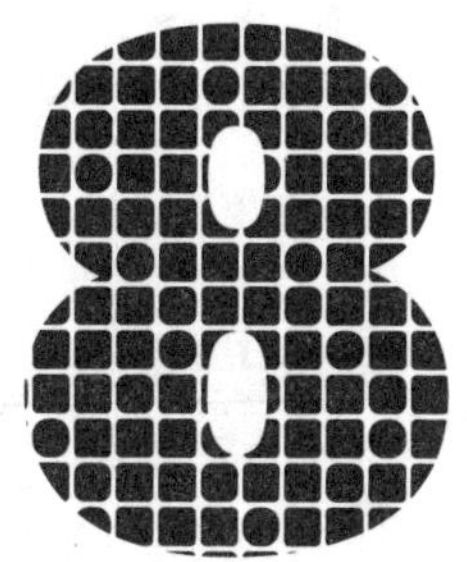

There's smoke in the kitchen when I get home that evening. Smoke and Sage.

The sec system is chirping, announcing, "Flames detected in the kitchen," and the front door is wide open, a steady stream of satin smoke diffusing into the evening air.

Embry stands by the front door with a dish towel in hand, encouraging the smoke to keep moving in the right direction.

He and Amethyst come over almost every night for no other reason than for us all to be together as a group. Their easy friendship both puts me on edge and makes me warm to see, especially the way they clearly love my sister. Even when she's starting kitchen fires.

"Who let her near the stove?" I ask, covering my nose and mouth before stepping inside.

Embry shrugs, but he's smiling. "Happened before I got here."

I can hear Sage issuing orders before I reach the kitchen. "Take it outside! No, not the garbage can, we've already started *one* fire."

"Who's this 'we' you're talking about?" Amethyst answers.

"It's the royal we," Sage counters. "Just put it in the grass or something."

"On the cement!" Tru adds. "Just set the whole tray on the patio. It'll be fine."

By the time I reach the kitchen, there's only Sage, fanning the air near the open oven with a look of stubborn desperation on her face.

"It wasn't my fault!" she shouts the instant she sees me. "I'm cursed, it's as simple as that."

Sage has taken on housemate duties with all her usual enthusiasm. She has a spreadsheet that charts out daily, weekly, and monthly chores, and she's assigned them to each of us on a rotating basis so that no one person ends up with the heaviest load or stuck with any particular chore. It has been painstakingly crafted for fairness and efficiency, and she won't budge on any of it. Not even taking her share of the cooking duties. And the only thing that my little sister is truly terrible at is cooking. It doesn't matter what it is, if there's the slightest chance it can be ruined, it will wither under her touch.

"It was just a frozen pizza!" she wails. "I don't know what I did wrong."

"It was probably the oven," Tru says as she and Amethyst return through the back door.

"I know you're just saying that," Sage says with a pout. "What are we going to do now? There's not another frozen pizza and everything else takes too long."

"It's already covered." Embry breezes into the room, cell phone in hand. "Our upgraded pizzas will be here in twenty minutes."

"Our hero," Amethyst teases.

"Look, I know my role is to spend my mother's money like she's not paying attention," he says, and the mention of Boss Acosta reignites the anger I've worked all day to smother.

"I wish she'd pay a little less attention to me," Tru mutters. "I have no idea what I'm supposed to wear tomorrow night. What are you wearing?"

"Something expensive that doesn't look expensive," he says. "I don't like to give anyone the impression that I want to be there. I don't even know why she's having the infamous Anderson Flynn over to begin with."

"Why does she want Tru there?" Sage asks with concern.

I'm behind on the conversation, but I don't have much trouble filling in the gaps. At some point today, after she was finished berating me, Boss Acosta designed a dinner party for Anderson Flynn. She wants her son there, which is understandable, and also Tru.

"To show her off, probably," Embry answers, jaded, but probably not entirely wrong.

"If half of what we've heard about this guy is true, it's smart," Amethyst adds.

"How so?" Sage asks.

"Because Tru is special and that makes her dangerous," I say, stepping forward to grab a bottle of water from the fridge. "The more Boss Acosta demonstrates her and Underhill, Inc.'s commitment to Tru, the safer she'll be."

"Because Anderson Flynn is as dangerous as they say?" Sage asks.

"Because it's best to assume he is," Amethyst clarifies.

"So you think my mom's doing this out of the goodness of her heart?" Embry asks, skeptical. "That doesn't sound right."

I laugh, probably a little harder than is called for. It's never been easy to imagine Boss Acosta doing much of anything out of the goodness of her heart, and after the past few days, it's pretty much impossible. But that's not the kind of thing I should say.

"I think it's more likely that she sees it as being in the best interest of Underhill," I say. "Though I also think that she wants to honor the promise she made to Tru. Your mom does strike me as a person of her word." Not to mention being exceptionally careful with the promises she makes.

Embry shrugs, filial wounds showing through the gesture, but he doesn't argue.

"Well, then," Sage says, sniffing primly. "I guess you should go, but I'm glad you'll be together. A lion's den is still a lion's den even if you're friends with the lion. Or the lion's cub, I guess."

Tru laughs warmly at her friend. "Where do you come up with this stuff?"

"I mean," Amethyst adds, "with those legs, don't you think he's more of a gazelle?"

"Must we continue to compare me to animals?" Embry asks, the smile on his face suggesting he doesn't actually mind.

Before anyone can respond, the sec system chimes and the automated voice issues from the panel on the wall next to the basement door, "Unidentified individual approaching the main entrance."

"Pizza already? That was fast," Tru says.

"I'll get it." Embry lopes out of the room on his long legs, doing nothing to counter the gazelle comparison. He returns only a few seconds later, empty-handed, or at least he seems to be.

"No pizza?" Sage asks.

"There was no one there," Embry answers. He holds up a small envelope between his thumb and forefinger. "Just a note for Tru."

At this distance, it looks like one of those tiny cards people attach to bouquets. Tru steps forward and takes the note from Embry. She slides the card out and reads the front, then, with a look of bafflement, flips it over to check the back. Her mouth drops open and she looks up in shock, racing toward the front door.

We hurry behind as she throws open the front door and runs out to the sidewalk, searching the street in both directions. But there's no one there.

"Tru? What's going on?" I ask. "What does it say?"

"I—I don't—" Tru stammers, still searching the empty streets.

"It says that Logan's alive," Embry supplies, having collected the note from where Tru dropped it in her haste.

"What?" Sage swipes the business card from Embry's grasp and reads both sides before turning it over to me.

It's just as plain as it appeared from a distance. On one side, there's a phone number printed in the middle; on the other, a handwritten note. It reads: *I know he's alive.*

The only "he" they could possibly mean is Logan. But it's the way it's written that catches my attention. It's written as if the only surprising thing is that someone *else* knows.

"He's alive?" I ask. "And you knew?"

Tru turns helpless eyes to me, the answer in them is plain.

"He's alive!" Sage rushes forward, flinging her arms around Tru's neck and hugging her. "That's amazing, Tru!"

Tru laughs a little, hugging Sage in return, but her eyes track back to mine, a question in them.

I wish I could be more like Sage sometimes. Not about most things and not all the time. Most of the time, I don't particularly want to share emotions the way Sage does. Moments like this are different.

I am hurt that Tru didn't tell me Logan was alive, but I can't blame her for keeping it secret. If anything, I admire her for it. It wasn't her secret to tell, and it speaks volumes that she kept his business private when I'm positive she wanted to share the good news with her friends. Maybe with me.

I'm also positive none of my complicated feelings are showing on my face, so I attempt a smile.

"Let's take this inside," Amethyst suggests, placing a hand on Tru's back and guiding her and Sage toward the house.

"How did you find out?" Sage asks before Embry shuts the door behind us.

"A text," Tru answers. "After everything was over, he let me know that he was safe, but he hasn't said anything since. I don't even know if he's in the city. I kind of hope he's gone to lie low somewhere far away and hard to reach like Greenland or Oklahoma or something." She returns her attention to the card in her hand, worry creasing her brow.

"So," Embry says when Tru has been quiet for a long moment. "Are you going to call the number?"

"What if it's a trap?" Sage asks.

"It's not a trap," I say. "It's an invitation."

"They already know where she lives," Amethyst points out. "If they wanted to spring a trap, they probably wouldn't ask for a phone call."

"It's the only way to find out what they want," Tru says, still staring at the card.

"Or what they know," I add.

Tru nods and pulls out her phone.

"Whoa, right now?" Sage jumps in alarm. "Hang on, hang on." She leaves the room and returns with a cereal bowl, which she sets on the coffee table in the middle of the room. "After you dial, set the phone in there so we can all hear. Amethyst, can you record on your phone? I know Tru could do it, but we don't want them to know we're recording them."

"Already on it," she answers, swiping at her screen.

Tru kneels by the coffee table, leaving room for the rest of us to crowd around, too. I settle in beside her and take her hand in mine, giving it a squeeze. She tries to smile in return, but it comes out as a nervous grimace.

"Okay," she says, blowing out a breath. Then she enters the number on the note, hits call, and puts it on speaker before setting the phone into the bowl.

It rings once, twice, and someone picks up halfway through the third.

Voices echo softly in the distance, the sound of footsteps on a hard surface, the shush of fabric, and then only breathing before "Gertrude?"

Tru swallows hard at the sound of her full name.

The voice is distorted by a vocal scrubber or perhaps an app that makes it hard to guess at a gender much less an age.

It seems they still want to hide even though they're the ones who sent the invite. Tru doesn't have that option, which is interesting—they clearly have something to lose if we learn who they are. Or they think they do.

It's something we can use to our advantage.

"Yes," Tru confirms, licking her lips. "Who is this?"

There's a touch of real fear in their tone when they answer, "I'd rather not say quite yet."

"Then what should I call you?" Tru counters.

There's a pause before they answer, "Let's go with Silver."

"Like the pirate?" Tru asks, then winces at her own joke. Referencing the notorious pirate from *Treasure Island* is definitely a unique kind of stress response. I squeeze her hand, wishing I could tell her it's okay to be nervous.

A laugh and then, "I do like to cook, so sure. Like the pirate." There's another brief pause before they continue. "I'm glad you called, Gertrude."

"Why?" Tru asks.

"You wouldn't have called if I was wrong. He's alive."

My stomach clenches. I should have realized. This was a fishing expedition. The card was the bait, and we all bit on it without an ounce of hesitation.

Shit.

No going back now.

"I assume so," Tru says, trying to keep her voice light.

"I think you've done more than assume," they say. "I'm not asking you to betray him, but I am glad to know he's well."

Embry slashes a hand through the air, shaking his head before Tru answers, but she catches it this time. She won't confirm or deny that she has any idea how Logan is.

"What is it you want from me?" she asks, changing course.

"A meeting," they say. "And before you ask why you should risk meeting with me in person, it is because I knew Logan a long time ago."

"A lot of people knew him," Tru counters smartly.

"A lot of people knew *of* him," they say. "But I knew *him*. And—" They hesitate. "I knew your mother."

Tru gasps, then clamps a hand over her mouth.

"And there are things I need to tell you, but not over the phone." Silver gives her a second, then continues talking about where and how they might meet, but I'm only half listening because Tru's eyes have moved out of focus, and I'm not sure she's hearing anything either.

I squeeze her hand again. She blinks, regaining her focus with a nod to let me know she's okay.

"I'm sorry," she says, stopping Silver in their tracks. "No."

"No? No, what?"

"I can't meet with you."

"I know how to find him," they say in a rush.

Tru's breath catches, but only for a second. I can see the raw desire in her face—this is something she wants, perhaps desperately, but she shakes her head.

"Not if he doesn't want to be found," she says, and then she ends the call.

The Third Explosion of Lila Morgan

Everything got better the older I got. It also got worse.

By the time I was a freshman at St. Isidor's, I figured out how to be a bombshell without ever using my talent. I also figured out how to be popular without having any real friends.

Both involved pretending.

I pretended that it didn't matter what I was.

I pretended I could control it.

I pretended that my friends liked me.

None of it was true. And I pretended that I wasn't angry about that fact all the time.

My father was also pretending, I think. That it would all be okay, that if he just tried hard enough, he could make it okay; that our family wasn't slowly cracking under the weight of our combined delusional anger and hope.

He also knew that the tightrope I was walking wasn't as sturdy as I believed. Eventually, it would give, and if I spent all my time and effort pretending the drop was a small one, it was going to kill me.

"We must practice, Lila," he said. "I know you're scared. I am, too, but that will only change with experience."

I knew he was scared. He couldn't hide the fear that haunted his eyes whenever he looked at me, so I knew he was telling the truth.

That didn't make it any easier when he told me to cancel my weekend plans because we were going back to that same field for practice.

"I hate you," I muttered as I texted an excuse to my friends for missing yet another sleepover.

"That's fine," he answered, sounding exhausted already. "Let's go."

It was spring and the heat was beginning to climb as we traveled to our middle-of-nowhere field. We spent the entire hour drive in silence, both of us indulging in our own thoughts and, in my case, irritations. By the time we arrived, my father was ready to talk.

"Lila," he began with a sigh. "I know you think that you can hold this inside forever, but I need you to believe me when I say you can't."

"I could have held it inside for one more night," I snapped.

"Maybe," he answered. "But with us, 'maybe' can get people killed."

"I feel fine!" I nearly shouted. "I'm not going to hurt anyone."

"Maybe," he repeated.

Enraged, I hopped out of the car and started to make my way into the tall grass. The sun dipped toward the horizon, and the field was a chorus of crickets and beetles and whatever else lived out there. A small copse of cottonwoods marked a spot in the near distance where a creek wended its way through the field. At its edge, a family of deer grazed the sweet spring grasses, occasionally raising their heads to listen for danger.

I aimed my steps for the trees and started walking away from my father.

"Lila," he called, hurrying behind. "The harder you work at suppressing your talent, the worse it will be when you do lose control."

"How do you know?" I challenged.

"Because I've tried," he answered. "Strongarms, bullseyes, wingtips, they're different. They can all ignore their talent if they want. They can get mad and careless, and it doesn't make a difference. We don't have that privilege."

"What privileges do we get?" I shouted back, hurrying forward.

"I"—he halted, sounding defeated—"I don't know how to answer that."

"That's because there are none! We get the privilege of being afraid of our own shadow! It's not fair!" I shouted, the warning note of my talent growing louder in my mind. "None of this is fair!"

"Lila," he said. This time it was a warning. "Deep breaths, Lila. Please."

"I don't want to take deep breaths, Dad! Isn't that why we're out here? So I can practice *not* taking deep breaths?!"

"Careful," he warned again. "Listen to me, you're spinning up too fast. You're going to hurt yourself."

"I don't *care*!"

I did care, but it was too late. I erupted then. The note inside me blasting at full strength before I knew what was happening. And I felt it all again—that exquisite explosion, that perfect oblivion, the realization of my bombshell talent.

It was incredible. Even if it hadn't been on purpose.

This time when I passed out, it only lasted a few moments. When I woke up, it was dusk. My father was kneeling several yards away, his focus on the ground.

I climbed to my feet, steps crunching over the singed grass that marked the radius of my explosion as I made my way to his side.

"This," he whispered, "is why we must be careful."

It took a moment for my eyes to register what I was seeing.

A fawn. With a coat of soft brown fur speckled with white dots, four lanky limbs stretched out long, and wide brown eyes. All of it still as the ground beneath my feet. Dead.

"I—" I started, horror thick in my throat.

I couldn't say the rest, but I felt it. The reality of what I'd done burrowed into my heart like a thorn. Grief and guilt brought so many tears to my eyes that I thought I might never stop crying.

My father didn't offer any platitudes and he didn't blame me. But I left the field that night knowing that everything I'd ever heard about bombshells was true. I was a dangerous weapon.

And I deserved to be alone.

"I can't believe how amazing Tru looked tonight and it wasn't to go on a date with you," Sage announces as she breaks into the bathroom while I'm taking a shower.

"No, I don't mind," I say. "Come in."

"I have to brush my teeth," she explains. "And I cannot believe you two haven't been on a real date yet. Do you know how weird that is? I mean, you live together but you don't have a favorite couples restaurant or anything like that."

"I'm aware," I say because life has taught me that ignoring Sage will only keep her in here with me longer.

"I lied, I'm going to pee, too," she adds. "But I won't flush."

The toilet lid clinks against the tank, and I hear Sage make good on her pronouncement. "Don't let me stop you," I say with a wry tone, but I kind of like this. Nothing makes me realize how seamlessly Sage fits into my life more than having her pee three feet away while I stand naked in the shower.

"I hope they're having an okay time," she muses. "They have each other so they'll be fine, but dinner with adults is just so boring. Can you imagine having to make small talk with someone like Anderson Flynn? Ugh."

"I'm sure they'll be fine."

"Do you think he has a spouse? Or, actually, I heard that he did have a daughter who died a long time ago," she continues, following her train of thought. "I think she was really young or something."

"She was," I say. This is one of the few stories I know about Anderson Flynn. "She was twelve, and it was a bounty that went wrong. She got caught in the cross fire."

"That's really sad," Sage says with real sympathy. "But still no excuse for being evil, I guess."

"I guess," I say, holding in my laughter at my sister's lightning emotional swings.

She falls silent for a minute, and I hear the toilet lid clink shut and the faucet come on as she washes her hands.

"You know what you should do? I mean, since it's been so long and all," she says, and I have no idea what she's talking about until she continues. "Take Tru to one of those fancy places on the plaza. Just take all the money you would have spent on five less formal dates and blow it on one. Steak, flowers, dessert, maybe even a ride on that new Ferris wheel, the whole nine yards. It would be so romantic."

For the first time in months, my bank account could almost handle a date like that, but my half of the bounty from Shin Splints is mostly spoken for between the balance on my credit card and covering our basic expenses, but Sage doesn't need to know that. In twenty-seven more days, I'll have my position at Ops back and no one will ever need to know.

"I'll take it under advisement. Any luck finding a summer job?" I ask, squirting shampoo into my hands and beginning to scrub my scalp.

"I turned in a few more applications," she says. "But I think I'll have better luck babysitting. There's a couple who wants a regular sitter for the whole month of July, and I think they'll hire me."

"How old is the kid?" I ask.

"They're five and seven," she answers, voice muffled now by a mouthful of toothpaste. "Easy-peasy."

Five and seven doesn't sound easy-peasy to me, but it is a decent fit for Sage's babysitting strengths, which boil down to anything but an actual baby.

"When will you know?"

"Soon. I think the deadline for applications is next week," she says. "I can check the app and let you know for sure, though." There's a pause before she adds, "We're okay, you know?"

My stomach pinches. "I know," I say. "But I want to make sure we stay that way."

I hear her sigh and then run the water to rinse her mouth,

and I know she uses my towel to dry her mouth because hers is hanging on the hook on the back of our shared bedroom door.

"I know you don't want to admit it, but I also know you're quietly panicking about, well, everything, but we *are* going to be okay. Everyone knows that none of what happened was your fault."

Even if that were true—and it's not—it wouldn't change anything. I'm still suspended, and Boss Acosta is watching my every move. But Sage, more than anyone else I've known, believes that people can be better than they are.

Which also isn't true.

But if I'm going to be a better version of myself for anyone, it's Sage. So, I bite my tongue and answer, "It only matters that you know that."

"Lila," she says in her parent voice. "It matters that *you* know that. Do you?"

I grit my teeth and scrunch up my whole face in a silent tantrum. And then I let it go.

"I know, Sage," I answer.

For one more second, she stays where she is. I know she's trying to decide if she's going to call me on that flat-out lie or let it be for another day. Mercifully, she chooses the latter.

"Good," she says with forced cheer. "I'll leave the closet light on for you, but turn it off before you go to bed, okay?"

"So, you're not staying up to pounce on Tru the minute she gets home?" I ask.

Sage laughs as though I've said the most ridiculous thing she's heard in an era. "Oh, I'm definitely going to pounce on her, but I'm tracking her phone. There's no reason I can't get a little presleep before she's back," she says.

"You are terrifying," I say.

And I can hear her smile when she answers, "Thank you."

There's a refreshing rush of cool air when she opens the door to leave. I turn off the shower and grab my towel, and by the time I reach our bedroom, Sage appears to be asleep with a pink satin eye mask on to block the soft light emanating from the closet. I flip it off and climb into bed next to her, then I pull out my phone and swipe to BountyApp.

The gold icon sporting the four interlocking circles that make up Underhill's insignia probably looks like a game or a mindfulness app to topsiders and anyone else unfamiliar with the hidden world of talented folk, but to us, it's everything. The login screen appears and it scans my face before letting me into my profile page, where my stats are listed:

NAME: *Lila Morgan*

MONIKER: *Sparrow*

TALENT: *Bombshell*

BOUNTIES CLAIMED: *96*

Monikers are used for anonymous bounties issued on an open call, when the priority is speed over all else. The sponsor who pays for an open-call bounty only sees the alias, never the name. But for bounties that prioritize a relationship between the client and the contractor, the client never sees the moniker: It's real names and by application only.

I flip to my list of open applications and my stomach turns over.

I've submitted more than a dozen applications in the past week. They've all been rejected. All thirteen are marked "read" and "passed."

Until two months ago, this had never happened to me before. I have an excellent track record. I've executed every bounty I've ever gone after, and I've claimed at least thirty-two open-call bounties in the past six months. I've done it all with speed, discretion, and efficiency. My reputation has always spoken for itself.

But that was before I fell beneath the long shadow of Ms. Jones and her actions.

Unbidden, Ryan's warning comes back to me, *They will pretend to trust you until the minute you do something they view as wrong, and then all bets are off.*

I drop my phone and squeeze my eyes shut. Sage may want to believe that people are better than their fears and demons, but they're not.

Frustration washes over me in violent waves. I know what I'm supposed to do. After my father lost control and killed all those innocent people, the only way I was able to survive was by ignoring what people said and focusing on myself. My actions, my words, my control, until I had gained a modicum of respect. But I was younger then, a ward of Underhill, not an adult trying to make a name for myself.

Ms. Jones would tell me that a bombshell's best weapon is her patience. Even after everything, I don't think she was wrong about that.

It's hardly comforting.

Sage shifts next to me, one foot stretching close enough to brush mine beneath the covers. What *is* comforting are my sister and my girlfriend and the fact that we all have a safe place to live. As much as I resist relying on other people, it feels good knowing I *can* rely on them. At least a little.

The rest, I will do the same way I've always done: on my own.

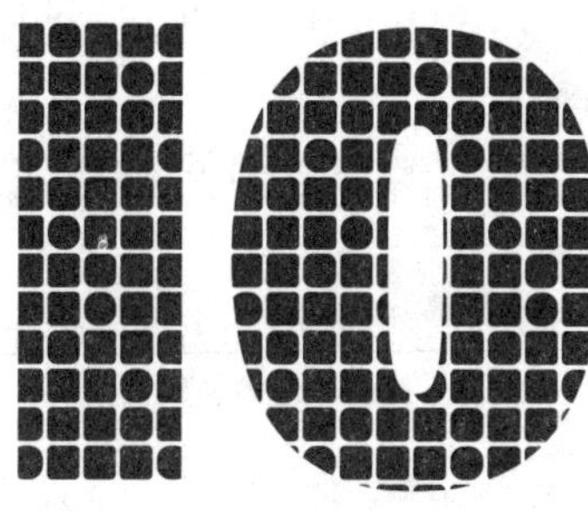

I'm not surprised when I learn that the whole crew is coming over for dinner the day after Tru and Embry dined with Boss Acosta and Anderson Flynn. There's probably a lot to unpack. But first, Tru sets me and Sage to work on dinner prep.

Tonight, the menu includes spaghetti with homemade pasta, and the kitchen smells incredible—tomatoes and onions and sweet fennel combine with the savory scent of sausage and the undercurrent of dough waiting to be pressed and stretched into noodles.

Despite Sage's insistence that she can handle stirring a pot, she's placed on salad duty and given the nearly foolproof task of chopping lettuce and vegetables while Tru and I tackle the sauce and noodles. I'm not great in the kitchen, honestly, but something about following Tru's steady instructions soothes me. She's done so much prep work that each step feels straightforward instead of the frenzied juggling act I'm used to.

Amethyst arrives first, joining the three of us in the kitchen, and in a move that's completely uncharacteristic, calls for our attention.

"I have an announcement and a request. I know we have a lot of other important things to discuss tonight so I just want to get this out of the way: I prefer he/him pronouns now and ask that you use them for me," he says, stripping off his pink satin bomber jacket and hanging it on the coatrack next to Tru's weighted vest. "He/him may not be right, but nothing has felt right for a while and I just need to try them."

It's probably the most I've ever heard Amethyst say in a single go, and I don't think I'm alone because for a moment, both Sage and Tru look completely taken aback.

But then Sage breaks into a grin. "That's awesome. Still Amethyst?"

Amethyst nods. "For now."

"Just let us know if that changes," Tru chimes in.

"Cool," Amethyst says. "Thanks."

Amethyst watches me with his cool gaze, his dark eyes the same tone as his earthy brown skin; his curls have grown out a bit and sit tight to his scalp.

I smile, letting him know that I'm on board, and he nods in response.

Apart from the little conversation we share in the sparring ring and what random bits Sage has shared over the years, I don't actually know that much about him. I only really know that he's thoughtful and seemingly unshakable. But I think that he always has a lot more going on beneath the surface. More than anyone will probably ever know.

I like that about him. I also like that when he needs something from his friends, he asks for it without making it feel heavy or burdensome.

"Any word from Embry?" Sage asks as she chops a carrot into wildly irregular pieces.

"He's been quiet all day," Amethyst reports. "But he said he might be late. There was something big going on at Underhill. I assumed it had something to do with whatever happened last night."

That's clearly directed at Tru, who shakes her head and then shrugs. "Nothing really happened last night," she says, letting a sheet of pasta dough fall back to the countertop. "It was just odd."

"Odd how?" Sage presses.

Tru frowns in the way she does when she's collecting her thoughts, one eye pinching tight. "Mr. Flynn was just kind of rude."

"To you?" Sage crosses the room in a sudden fury, brandishing the knife near Tru's face. If Tru were anyone else in the world, it would be too close for comfort.

"A little. Embry was actually more upset about it than I was, but Flynn demanded a demonstration of my talent," Tru says, still clearly uncomfortable by the memory.

"Did you give him one?" I ask, horrified.

Tru nods. "I wasn't sure what else to do, and he spent

the rest of the night talking in vague terms about 'dangerous talents.'"

"Sounds like a reason for an impromptu meeting at Underhill to me," Amethyst says, moving to take the knife from Sage and finish chopping the carrots himself.

"But why would Embry have to be there?" Tru asks. "He actively tries to avoid official Underhill stuff."

"He usually does." Amethyst turns to face me. "Were you in Underhill today? Did you hear about this meeting?"

I feel this for the invitation it is—this is the moment to tell them that Boss Acosta hasn't lifted my suspension, that for the past few days when I leave the house, I only pretend to go to work when I'm really searching for bounties to make ends meet. I should be like Amethyst and simply say what I need. But I don't actually know what I need, and maybe that's the real problem.

"No," I say, clearing my throat. "I wasn't invited."

I catch Tru and Sage locking eyes for a split second, the tension that passes between them, and the almost imperceptible shake of Sage's head.

So, maybe they've figured out more than I thought.

"Hopefully Embry will know more," Sage admits.

"I might," Embry announces. A second later, he appears in the doorway of the kitchen looking lean and elegant with Thea balanced on one hip. He's dressed in a moss-green, floor-length skirt with a black vest pulled tight over a white button-down, his big brown eyes narrowed with anger as he sweeps into the room.

"But I'm afraid it's not good news," he says, casting a firm look toward me.

Thea squirms to be let down and instantly charges across the room to wrap her arms around Tru's legs. The time they spent together evading deadly assassins left an indelible bond between them. Even though she lives with Embry and his mom, she's over here often enough that we have a growing stash of toys and an impressive collection of clothes.

Thea gives a happy little growl and raises her arms. "Up, up, up," she says, and Tru softens, bending down to scoop her up.

"Maybe we should sit down?" Sage suggests.

Everyone turns to me. Waiting for me to make the first move or be a delicate flower or something. "Just say it, Embry."

Embry crosses his arms over his chest. "The council met today to discuss new Underhill legislation about bombshells."

"Legislation?" Amethyst asks at the same moment Sage asks, "Bombshells?"

I can feel Tru's eyes on me, but I've turned solid and cold, the frozen surface of a lake.

"They're putting a new requirement in place." Embry lowers his eyes to the floor and recites from memory, "'Starting today, no bombshell will be allowed to work without the presence of an approved partner.'"

"That's bullshit!" Sage explodes, causing Thea to jump in Tru's arms. "They can't do that!"

"They can," Embry answers. "And they did."

"What does 'approved partner' mean?" Amethyst asks.

"I'm not sure," he admits.

"Is this a permanent change?" Tru asks. "Or temporary?"

"Does it matter?" Sage is so mad, she's practically spitting. "Did you argue against it?" Sage demands, her blue eyes sparkling with rage as she rounds on Embry.

"I don't exactly have a voice at the table," he says.

"But did you even try?"

"It's not his fault," I say.

"I didn't say it was, but I want to know if you just sat there while they stripped away my sister's rights. Did you sit next to your mom like a good boy?"

At that, Embry snaps. "Of course, I didn't! I told them that this was a bad idea. Not only because it turns bombshells into second-class citizens, but because it will ultimately drive people away from Underhill, into a lawlessness that history has shown us leads to abuses of all kinds, and isn't that exactly what we *don't* want to happen?" Embry presses a hand to his chest, breathing hard.

Sage takes a small step back, the vibrant edge of her anger already fading. "I'm sorry. Of course you didn't just sit there."

"It didn't matter. Someone had a video of two bombshells having a fight near Southwest Boulevard the other night, and that was essentially case open and closed." Embry takes a steadying breath and shakes his head. "There's more."

The room stills, bracing for impact.

Embry purses his lips as though the words are unbearably bitter. "They are going to require that bombshells wear a pulse monitor at all times."

The room erupts again. In a distant, calm part of my brain,

I can distinguish Sage's shouts from Tru's alto and Amethyst's quiet and modest responses, but it's all just noise, background to the chemical spike of adrenaline that sends my heart rate skyrocketing. I have the bitter thought that it's a good thing I'm not wearing a pulse monitor yet.

It takes a minute for my ears to clear and when they do, I realize Embry has started speaking again. "They're drafting the official paperwork now. I expect there will be an announcement first thing in the morning."

I wonder if they'll use the video as evidence, or if they'll even need to. I wonder how much worse this can all get, and then I hope I never have to find out.

I've hardly finished the thought when our phones issue a collective chime. Numbness washes over me when I open BountyApp and tap on the news alert.

They didn't wait until morning.

It's a memo with more words than I care to read, but I get the gist and the bottom line is an order: All bombshell talents must report to Underhill, Inc., before 6 p.m. tomorrow to receive and acknowledge these new regulations.

"Lila?" Tru asks, and Thea echoes the name in her own way, "La-La."

Waves of emotions roil through me. Anger giving way to sorrow, shame morphing into disgust, all of it real and none of it particularly useful.

The kitchen has fallen silent but for the thick bubble of spaghetti sauce on the stove and Thea's nervous chirping. I see Tru start to lower Thea to the ground, her body listing toward me as though she might try to touch me. As though she doesn't understand that I will fracture and fall apart if she tries. I move before she can, crossing the room to get out of it.

When I reach the doorway, I pause and without turning to look at them—because I cannot bear to see the sympathy and sympathetic rage in their eyes right now—I say, "I just need a minute to myself. Please . . . please don't follow me."

I hate crying. Nothing makes me feel less in control than the urgent press of tears in my eyes, or the way sobs billow up from the very root of me, unbidden. Crying is as violent as a storm and there's nothing to do but ride it out.

The best way to avoid it is to stop it before it begins.

Clamping my jaw against the pressure, I grab my windbreaker from where I hung it on the coatrack, then slip out the front door as quietly as I can. The sec system will log my departure, but I don't need to be invisible. Just quiet enough to get away before anyone has a chance to comfort me.

The way Tru looked at me just now. Sympathy and defensive anger merging into something powerful and determined on her face . . .

The thought of dealing with everybody else's feelings—even if their anger and fear are on my behalf, maybe *especially* if they're on my behalf—makes my skin prickle. Because as much as I know they love me and care about me, none of them can understand what this feels like.

They will try. And when I am less angry, I won't mind, but right now I can't pretend that our experiences have parallels.

I hit the sidewalk and turn left because I almost always turn right when I leave for my morning run. After that, I don't pay attention to my route. I just walk beneath the orange streetlights and seethe until I no longer feel like I'm carrying a hurricane inside me. Only a gentle thunderstorm.

I don't expect the world to be fair—I expect it to demand something it calls fairness of me and never offer it in return—but sometime in the past two years, I tricked myself into expecting respect. I fooled myself into thinking that my actions and work would be noticed; that I would be judged based on the merits of my work and not only my talent. That I would not be punished for the actions of others.

Yet, here I am. Bound by rules that do not apply to others, rules designed out of fear and that do nothing to help bombshells, when we are already bending over backward to make others feel comfortable.

It would be funny if it wasn't also so serious. Yes, I have more than one person in my life who will join me on a bounty the moment I ask them to. The point is, I shouldn't have to.

Just like the strongarms and wingtips and bullseyes don't have to. Not even Tru has faced this kind of restriction, and two months ago, "bastion" was the equivalent of a curse word.

Ryan's words come back to me: *If you ever get tired of playing by their rules, give me a call.*

I stop walking long enough to pull my wallet from my pocket and find his card, then I punch in the number and send a text:

> *I'm ready.*

A few seconds pass before his response appears.

> *Meet me at the riverfront. I'll be there in ten.*

It's followed by a mapped location, but I know the place, and my rage-walking has taken me halfway there already. I respond with a thumbs-up, then cut over to the KC Streetcar line and catch one headed in the right direction.

The trip takes just over ten minutes. I use the time to send messages to Tru and Sage telling them I went out and not to worry, and then I turn my notifications off.

Ryan is waiting for me at the riverfront. He leans back against the railing of the overlook where the fence is studded with padlocks. A single streetlight overhead throws long shadows down his pale cheeks, but I can see that he's smiling.

"Not a fan of the new regs?" he asks. I don't answer, but he's not really expecting me to. "C'mon," he says, pushing off the railing and leading me down the stairs to the walking path below.

Long chain-link fences block access to the river, and we walk along in silence for a while before he steps off the path and into the thick brush between us and the fence. I hear the note of his talent a second before I feel heat radiating from his hands. He raises one softly glowing hand and drags it down the length of the fence, peeling back the chain-link to let us through.

"That's vandalism," I point out.

"I'll weld it shut again when we leave," he says breezily, and it takes me a second to realize he means with his talent. In public. "It won't be as pretty, but it'll be just as strong."

"What are we doing here?" I ask as he charts a path toward the river.

"Swimming," he says with a mischievous grin tossed over one shoulder.

Ahead, the river glides along its way, a glossy gray-brown ribbon beneath a night sky illuminated by the lights of the city. Crickets and frogs sing around us as we travel deeper into the early summer brush.

I usually wouldn't go off-roading like this. I like nature well enough, but I prefer it with a marked path and a low risk of ticks or poisonous snakes, but tonight I find that I don't mind at all.

When we reach the bank of the river, Ryan wastes no time stripping off his shirt and pants, leaving only his boxers in place and putting his shoes back on. In the moonlight, his pale skin seems to glow, and I can't help but notice the cut of muscle on his abdomen before I avert my eyes.

"Are you going in wearing all of that?" he asks, gesturing

to my clothing. "I don't recommend it. Well, except for shoes. You never know what people have thrown in there."

"I thought you were joking," I say, suddenly self-conscious at the prospect of stripping down to my bra and underwear with someone I hardly know.

"I was not," he says. "But I'll turn my back if it makes you feel better?"

"I have a girlfriend," I say, cheeks warming.

"I know," he says with humor. "And don't take this the wrong way, but you're not my type. I told you to call me if you wanted to break the rules, not for a date."

My cheeks heat even more, and I'm glad it's dark enough to hide a radioactive blush. "Turn around," I say.

He complies, and I strip down to my underthings and shoes, then hurry into the water.

The riverbed is softer than I expected, and I sink in to my ankles with each step until I'm deep enough to swim. Ryan is right behind me, and together we swim until we're in the middle of the river.

For a moment, I take in the sight of it. The stark white cables of the Bond Bridge driving up to a point in the distance, the lights of the city glittering atop the hill, and in the opposite direction, the hulking shadows of the West Bottoms, where the river curls away into the rolling prairie. It's a view of the city I've never seen before, quiet and lovely and enough that I can almost forget what drove me out here in the first place.

"Okay, we're going to dive," Ryan says, treading water next

to me. "And then we're going to give ourselves to the song."

"The song," I repeat. "Do we all hear the same one?"

"In a way." The smile he offers me is beatific. "But when you throttle it the way you've been doing, it's really nothing more than noise and chaos. All the component parts are there, but they're out of balance. Which is why so many Underhill bombshells ultimately explode in the bad way."

"Okay, so what do I do about it?" I ask. "What's your mysterious, non-Underhill method?"

"We're going to work on adjusting the volume. Up and down."

I almost roll my eyes. "What do you think I've spent my life doing? I know how to use my talent."

"No offense, but if that were true, you wouldn't be here." He gives me a smile that's almost apologetic.

I swallow hard against my pride. Because he's right.

"So," he continues, "you've been taught that your talent has a switch that you can turn on or off. But that's never been true. Your talent is always there. Always on, and if you want to use it the way it was meant to be used, you need to learn how to adjust the volume. We're going to turn it up as high as you're comfortable going and then back down."

"You're sure we won't hurt anyone?" I ask.

"Maybe some fish," he admits. "But the river barges don't run at night and the water is deep here. Deep enough to provide cushion."

"And what about us?" I ask. "Turning the volume up that far will knock me out. Won't it do the same to you? We'll drown."

But he shakes his head. "There's a difference between letting the song tear through you like a wildfire and turning the volume up. Think of this more like a controlled burn."

The muscles in my arms and legs warm as I tread, but that's not why I'm suddenly short of breath. Yes, I called Ryan to break the rules, but doing something like this in public—even underwater—still feels wrong. It feels dangerous.

"I don't think I can do this," I say, shaking my head.

"You're afraid," he says without any hint of judgment.

"I'm afraid," I confirm.

He purses his lips in thought. For a moment we tread water to the distant sounds of the city, horns blaring and sirens wailing and the steady beat of a concert from the Power and Light. Then he catches one of my wrists, stopping the movement of my arm.

"Can you float?" he asks, and when I nod, he lets me go and tips back against the surface of the water.

I follow suit, letting my body relax and drift up until I'm floating alongside Ryan, traveling down the river like a fallen leaf.

"You feel that?" he asks, voice muffled by the water in my ears. "How we've joined the current?"

"I do." I flutter my hands a bit to stay horizontal.

"How we don't have to fight it to be a part of it?" he continues. "It only surges when it's been blocked or dammed somewhere upstream. But when it's allowed to flow, it has a natural rhythm. It's the same with the song. We can slip in and out at will, without losing ourselves."

"Okay, I get it," I say. "And if we don't stop flowing soon, we're never going to find our clothes again."

He laughs, but he stops, turning to face me as he treads water. "You want to give it a try?"

My nerves spike, but I pull in a deep breath. The earthy sweet scent of river water fills my lungs. "Yes," I say.

"Then let's go." He takes my hand in his and, with a final gulp of air, dives beneath the surface.

He doesn't let go, so I have no choice but to fill my own lungs and dive alongside him.

I keep my eyes closed because river water is not the sort of thing I want to invite inside my body in any fashion. His hand is warm and firm in mine. We pull with our free arms to help us go even lower, and then I hear the first faint notes of a melody seeming to echo from somewhere far away.

It teases at the edges of my mind, testing and tempting until I can't resist letting my own notes play alongside it. I feel Ryan's hand grip mine with more strength as though telling me it's okay to let go.

Before tonight, I would have resisted. Too afraid of being caught to take the risk. But tonight, I can't bring myself to care about being caught. Judgment has been cast regardless.

Tonight I need to know what I'm capable of. So I make myself relax the grip I maintain on the song inside of me, and I turn the volume up.

It climbs, and another song—it can only be Ryan's—climbs with it. Braiding around each other to create a new, more complex yet somehow simultaneously simple melody that sings through my bones. It grows and grows, never catapulting ahead the way I was afraid it would, but driving forward playfully, two horses galloping across a field.

Heat builds in my chest and I'm vaguely aware that I should be starving for air, but everything hums and vibrates around me in the most delicious way. My head spins like I've had a sip of bubbly champagne, yet I can still hear myself. I can think with clarity and coherence, and that realization is at once relieving and so heady.

The song grows again, surging like the river. Driving toward a familiar point where I lose all sense of myself. My stomach lurches and I begin to count, to defuse the bomb that is me before explosion is inevitable.

But then Ryan's other hand is in mine. He holds me there, in the dark of the river, his hands firm and just as hot as my own, reminding me that I am not alone. And he has been here before.

Together, we become a chord resonating with heat and energy. I feel electric and insubstantial, like I could become that terrible supernova at any second. But like it would be my choice. Like it isn't inevitable.

And with that thought, I begin to turn the volume back down.

The energy I've built dissipates into the river bit by bit until it's just me again, and I climb to the surface.

When I open my eyes, Ryan is there. Head bobbing so that his mouth is hidden in the water, but I can tell that he's smiling.

And I am, too. Smiling in a way that I can't remember ever smiling before. I feel light and effervescent and euphoric, like laughter given form. But it's fleeting, and soon I'm me again and it's late enough that I should really be getting home.

Ryan doesn't say anything as we head back to shore and hunt for the spot where we left our clothes. He doesn't make me admit that this was exactly what I needed or tell him how it made me feel. I'm grateful, but the longer we pass in silence, the heavier I feel.

This was temporary. A hidden moment that I cannot share with anyone without making them complicit. Because no one trusts a bomb not to go off, and I can't ask someone to stay quiet about watching me light the fuse.

Ryan must have sensed the shift in my mood, because once we're dressed, he catches my hand. I hear the wisp of a song—his—stirring in the space between us.

"You don't have to let them decide who you are," he says.

I know he's right. I only wish it mattered. "They'll do it anyway," I say. I can see the glimmer of disappointment in his face, but he doesn't argue, and I think I might truly like him.

I head back to the path, pausing there to watch him weld the fence closed with a glowing hand, his easy freedom making me feel more trapped than ever.

When he joins me on the path, I do my best to give him a real smile. "Thanks for this. I appreciate it."

"Any time," he answers.

And then, before I go, I ask, "What is your boss doing in town?"

If Ryan is surprised by the change in topic, he doesn't let on. He shrugs. "I'm sure you understand that even if I did know about any plans he may or may not have, I wouldn't tell you." He bends to look me directly in the eye when he adds, "Because that would be supremely ill-advised."

It's a reminder that his boss isn't as murder averse as mine. He may have fewer restrictions on using his talent, but we are both bound by our loyalties.

"What's his obsession with bastions?" I ask, taking a different tack.

Ryan blinks, revealing more than he meant to. "Who said—"

"He did," I cut in, because when you have someone off their game, you keep them off. "Twice. He interrogated Boss Acosta about bastions the minute he got to town, and he questioned Tru in front of an entire dinner party last night."

"I think everyone has questions about bastions these days," Ryan says, hedging. "Don't you?"

I watch him closely, searching for anything that might tip his hand. But he's given away all he's going to.

"Don't worry," he adds, flashing that charming smile. "I'm sure my boss has bigger fish to fry than your girlfriend."

I'm pretty sure he meant to be reassuring, but all I hear is a threat.

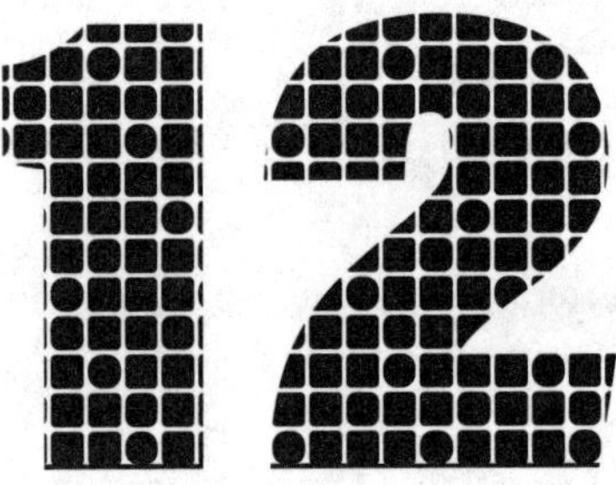

My pulse monitor—compliments of Underhill's finest minds—is essentially a smartwatch. It has a matte black display face, black band, and black trim and I hate it. They pull it snug against my skin before snapping it on, and as far as I can tell, there's no way for me to remove it without cutting the band.

I'd wanted to do this alone, but Sage predicted my attempt to sneak out. By the time I'd made it downstairs, all four of them were gathered around the kitchen table, looking wan over cups of coffee.

Arguing seemed like more battle than I had in me today, so I'd entered Underhill escorted by a phalanx of people with absolutely no power to do anything other than look on while

I was read my new rights, or lack thereof, and tagged like a criminal.

I think it upset Embry the most. He's still prowling around the house hours later, alternately muttering about finding a way to disable it and throwing all his focus into his laptop. Amethyst works steadily by his side, seeming to anticipate what he'll need when, even if *what* involves physics. Meanwhile, Tru is baking up a storm in the kitchen and Sage is getting in her way.

It's too much, so in one of the rare moments when Tru isn't holding something hot or sharp, I pull her aside and ask if she'd like to go to a movie.

"Wha— I'm— I mean . . ." she stammers, mouth falling open before she recovers. "Right now?"

I nod, amused because of the two of us, no one would ever peg me as the spontaneous one. "I would really love to take you on a date right now."

Sage appears just behind Tru, pushing up onto her toes so she can hiss into her ear, "Say yes!"

Tru's cheeks tinge pink, but she laughs. "Yes, okay. Just— give me like five minutes to get the galette out of the oven and change into something that doesn't smell like dough."

"I'll find a movie," I say. "Any requests?"

"Something sci-fi or scary, but not too scary," she answers, hurrying out of the kitchen.

Twenty minutes later, we're in line for a comically sized bucket of popcorn and equally ridiculous cups of soda at a theater on Ward Parkway. There's hardly anyone here because it's the beginning of the week and middle of the day, and the lobby feels cavernous and empty and like we're doing something we shouldn't, but at least I don't have to worry about who is or isn't noticing the metaphorical scarlet letter around my wrist.

We find our theater and seats and settle into the plush recliners, putting the footrests up until our heads tip back. Advertisements play on the screen as we wait for the movie to begin—there was an alien in the poster so I'm pretty sure it meets Tru's requirements, but this is not my area of expertise.

"Looks like we're going to have the whole place to ourselves," Tru whispers, leaning into the little armrest that separates our seats.

"I can't remember the last time I came to a theater," I say. "Did you and Papa Stallard do this often?"

Tru laughs, the sound carrying into the dimly lit room like a little song. "I can't really imagine what he'd have done in a place like this. Actually, I can. He'd have spent the whole movie tracking all movement in and out of the theater, and by the end, he'd have found some way to sneak away from me. He'd plant himself somewhere and wait to see if I noticed him in time to prevent or subvert the attack."

She sits up to survey the room more completely.

"There," she says, pointing to the place where the facade of the wall ends, dividing the room from the exiting hallway. "He would know that that's where I'd expect him to be so he would hide"—she narrows her eyes, then points—"right there.

At the far end of the room, where he'd have a clear line of sight and could come up behind me without making a sound."

"That does not sound like the way most people enjoy movies." I'm actually a little alarmed by this glimpse into Tru's childhood. I was always on my guard, but this is next level.

I spent years thinking of Tru as just another talented kid, watching her for any sign that she might mean Sage harm. I only ever looked at her for what I feared she might be, and, I'm coming to realize, for what she wanted me to see. I'm still getting used to this new version of her.

She shrugs. "I got used to it, and in fairness to him, it *was* by request. Can't really blame a deadly assassin for being deadly in the service of training another deadly assassin."

"I guess not," I say, watching the way Tru's smile softens. With sadness, I think, but also with longing. "You must miss him," I say.

"Yeah." She bobs her head, then tucks her chin to get a sip of her Cherry Coke.

"You don't have to talk about it if you don't want to," I say, reaching out and resting my hand on hers. "But you can."

When she lifts her gaze back to mine, I'm surprised by the sympathy I find there.

"Lila," she says. "I'm the one who should be comforting you right now."

My eyes fall to the band on my wrist. I truly regret that it's summer and the thought of long sleeves is unbearable.

"I don't need comfort," I answer sharply. "I don't actually know what I need, but I *want* to pretend none of this is happening. At least until we go back home and Sage makes that impossible."

"Or Embry," Tru adds. "We might need to sedate him."

"I didn't know he had so much . . ." I hesitate, searching for the right words. Like Tru and Amethyst, I didn't really know Embry before a few months ago, but unlike them, I can't really claim to know him now. Before, all I had were impressions and reservations centering around Sage. Now I'm learning that he has far more depth and dimension than I'd realized. "Range of emotion," I finish.

Tru laughs softly, fondly, her mind traveling to her friends. "He really struggles with who his mom is and what she does, but I think it's because he loves her so much."

"I can empathize with that," I say.

"Me too," Tru adds. She falls silent for a minute, slowly bobbing her straw up and down so the ice churns in her cup.

Another couple walks in and we both watch them without seeming to, our eyes tracking their steps as they search for their seats two rows above ours. They vanish from view, but I'm willing to bet Tru knows as well as I do that they're seated directly behind us.

"I don't know why he hasn't contacted me again," she says after a long moment, so softly her voice is almost lost beneath the swell of music announcing the start of the previews. "Do you think I did something wrong?"

"You haven't done anything wrong," I answer automatically. "You saved Boss Acosta's life, not to mention all of Underhill from some pretty extensive damage. And you did all that at great cost to yourself and your well-being. There's no way he'd be upset with you for that."

The frown on Tru's face tells me that she's considered this precise argument and rejected it.

"What is it?" I press.

"Underhill," she says. "He left Underhill to protect my life, and I turned around and joined it. After they put a kill bounty on his head."

The previews roll on as I consider this, the volume of screams and crashes and pulse-pounding music easily covering our conversation.

"I didn't know him," I start, shifting so that I can catch her hands more fully in mine. "But based on what I do know—how he took you in, cared for you, and taught you to be strong and smart and safe—I don't think he's the kind of person who would hold a grudge against someone he loved. Loves."

Tru's eyes turn glossy and bright, glimmering in the flashes of movie light as she blinks back tears.

"Am I wrong?" I ask.

She shakes her head. "No, you're not wrong. I just—I miss him and I don't understand why he won't come back."

"Maybe there's a reason," I suggest. "Something you don't know about."

She stares at me. "You think he's in trouble."

I give her a slow nod.

"And he doesn't want me to get involved?" she asks.

I nod again. "What parent would?"

She nods, but she's not looking at me anymore. I can see

her mind working furiously to draw connections out of precious little information, and I see the moment she lands on the same thing I have.

"Silver," she says.

"Silver," I repeat.

"We should contact them," Tru says, squeezing my hands. "Tonight."

"Shhh!" The command comes from two rows above and draws our attention to the fact that the movie has started.

"Tonight," I whisper, grinning to see Tru so eager.

Then she does something I do not expect. She leans in, sliding one hand along my jaw into my hair, and she pulls my head forward until our lips meet.

And. I. Am. Liquid.

Heat rushes through me, billowing up and down and through until I simmer inside and out. The drop in my stomach is delicious as Tru deepens the kiss, takes command, and I seem to be dissolving everywhere except the points where she's touching me—the back of my neck, my lips, the featherlight brush of the fingers on her other hand against my forearm. The quick, pulsing buzz against my wrist.

My wrist.

I pull away and jump to my feet. My breath is quick, my skin hot, my pulse a staccato beat in my veins. Whatever Tru is saying to me, I don't hear it. I just run.

Out of the theater, down the hall, past the two staff members who definitely don't seem alarmed at the sight of a girl fleeing their place of work, out into the humid air and blaring sunlight.

I stop there, panic dropping like a spear from the crown of my head to my toes. All I can think about is my father. Perfectly, completely in control one day, a smear on the street the next. A volatile, careless murderer.

The monitor at my wrist continues buzzing its alarm. *Zap-zap-zap.*

I struggle to remember what the tech said. Something about a feedback loop and degrees of warning, but it's a meaningless jumble in my mind. The only coherent thought I have is that I should get away from here.

"Lila!" Tru shouts, cutting through everything else.

I spin, one hand held out to her, even though a small, desperate part of my mind reminds me that I cannot hurt her. Unlike everyone else in my life, she can survive me.

"Stay away," I say around gasping breaths. "It's—my monitor, it's—"

"Lila." Tru's voice softens. She takes a step toward me. "It's not you. Well, I mean, it's not your talent."

"But—" I draw in a deep breath and feel my heart begin to slow and I realize something else: There's no song, no hum, no electric heat building in my body. She's right. It's not my talent.

Tru's smile turns sheepish and sweet. She takes another step forward.

The buzzing at my wrist slows with my heart and, from one second to the next, stops altogether.

"Oh my god," I murmur, embarrassment settling over me like a weighted blanket.

"I think it's kind of romantic," Tru says, stepping close. "But only in a really annoying, authoritarian-government-is-always-watching kind of way."

"You know they're on their way," I say. I remember that much from this morning: Any moment, there will be an Underhill task force coming to stop the big bad bombshell. "I'm sorry but I think I've ruined our date."

But Tru only shrugs and takes a seat on the steps. "Let's just say that the outcome we got is different from the one we expected."

I spot the cars as they peel off of Ward Parkway and cut through the parking lot like it's an obstacle course. I take a seat next to Tru and wait for the cavalry to arrive.

"Okay," I say. "Let's go with that. But we're going to need a different story for Sage."

The calvary arrives in a nondescript gray sedan. It doesn't make an impression the way a fleet of fresh-off-the-lot black SUVs does. Underhill prefers to buy up boring cars in all the colors you'd find in a bowl of oatmeal and fly under the radar.

Not one but three figures emerge from the car and approach me, spreading out as though I'm a flight risk. Or a live bomb.

"Miss," the middle one says, looking at Tru. "Please step away."

"No, thank you," Tru answers, meeting his urgency with politeness. "I'm fine where I am."

"We're not here to hurt anyone," he continues, inching closer while his teammates do the same on either side of me.

"We're from the Bombshell Containment Task Force and we're here to help, but I need you to please clear the area."

His hand is clenched around an unfamiliar object. It's small, cylindrical, and reflects the light like glass, just like the crystals that make up the protective columns in the practice rooms at Underhill, but much smaller. I've never heard of a portable containment field, but it's not much of a leap to conclude that's the idea. A glance over each shoulder confirms that the other two goons have similar devices, and that they are spaced out behind me, putting me in the center of a triangle with crystals at each point.

"I'm not active," I say, getting to my feet.

"Just stay right there!" The one in front of me raises his voice, his body dipping into a defensive crouch as though I've just done something to threaten him.

"Hey," Tru says, waving a hand through the air. "She just said she's not active. You can . . . stand down or whatever. If you're tracking her so well, don't you have something that can confirm what she's saying?"

He pauses long enough to check his phone, studying something that I can't see, but probably has everything to do with me.

He glances back up, tentative, as if reluctant to believe what his device, his eyes, and my words are all telling him.

"State your name, please," he commands.

"Lila Morgan," I say, making my voice frost, my body ice. Nothing but cool and calm.

He takes another step forward and Tru moves, too, placing herself almost fully between us. The man's mouth pulls tight, but he keeps his focus on me.

"Lila Morgan, I'm John Marshall, BCTF lead. We received an alert from your monitor. Can you tell us why that might be?"

I do not want to tell this guy why my heart rate spiked just a few moments ago.

"Probably because this new system was thrown together too quickly and doesn't allow room for bombshells to also be human?" Tru says.

"I really am going to have to ask you to step aside, Miss." He rounds on Tru, reaching out to usher her away without actually touching her.

"Miss, if you could come with me," another one of these trolls says, attaching themselves to Tru. "The faster we can get a statement, the faster this will be over with and you can both be on your way."

I can hear Tru arguing quietly behind me, but I keep my attention on John Marshall, BCTF lead. He's about ten years older than me with early wrinkles lining the tanned skin of his forehead and eyes, and blond hair starting to thin around the temples.

He watches me with a hint of smug expectation, as though he anticipated being here. As though he knows I've done something wrong.

"You wanna tell me what really happened, Miss Morgan?" he asks.

"Nothing happened," I say. I know he's waiting for more, but I don't have to tell him anything more. What I've just said is the absolute truth as far as he's concerned.

"Nothing?" he asks, disbelieving. "C'mon, it's okay if you started to lose control for a second. It doesn't make you a bad bombshell, but I do have to record the incident. I have to put something down."

"You could let them know it was an error," I suggest.

He doesn't like that at all. I can see it in the humorless smile that stretches his mouth.

"Like I said," he starts again. "I have to put something down, so help me out a little or I'll have to say that you were uncooperative. And I don't think that will end up looking very good for you."

I smother the anger that sparks in my chest. Tru is still arguing with the other two members of the task force. I don't have to hear a word she says to know she's defending me. She will defend me no matter what happens here.

"We're doing this for everyone's safety," John continues, taking my silence for hesitation instead of the refusal it is. "I know you want to help us help everyone. I just need to know what happened to make you activate."

"And I told you, I didn't activate," I answer without any hint of emotion. "This thing tracks my heart rate, because it's a proxy for my talent. It also happens to be a normal function of the human body. I can't be any more helpful than that."

The empty smile on his face rots in place, revealing the staid disgust it had never quite managed to hide.

He taps at his screen for a few moments before turning it to face me, all trace of his previous civility gone. "Place your thumb in the square at the bottom to indicate you've reviewed this report. A copy will be sent to you and placed on file with Underhill, Inc. If you disagree with the report, details on how to appeal will be included with the copy that is sent to you."

I hold my hand out for his screen and stare at him until he reluctantly lets me take it. Big red letters read Potential Activation Incident above a coded explanation that records my insistence that the reading was mistaken or a result of something else. I take my time reading it, and only when I'm sure every word is accurate do I press my thumb to the bottom of the screen.

He takes it back with more force than is called for.

"Thank you, Miss Morgan," he says. "Have a good rest of your day."

A slick, oily feeling settles over me as I watch him and his goons pull away from the curb. There aren't many bombshells in the city and now there's a task force dedicated to monitoring us. It's a self-fulfilling prophecy. It won't be long before the additional pressure of so many eyes on us leads to something terrible. A watched bombshell goes off. Eventually.

"This is not good," Tru breathes when the car is finally out of sight. "We have to do something."

I nod. "We're going to contact Silver and find out what they think they know."

Tru turns to face me, searching. "I think I've lost the thread. What does Silver have to do with any of this?"

"Nothing, as far as I know," I say. "This is all just a distraction. It's frustrating and unfair and there's no way it can last, but Logan is none of those things. So let's keep our eyes on what's important and find out what Silver knows. Okay?"

"Okay," she says slowly. "But we're still going to have to come up with a story for Sage because we can*not* tell her what just happened."

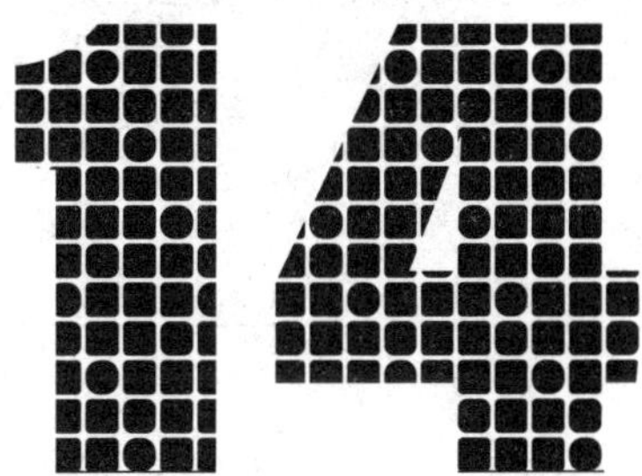

For having spent nearly the last decade of her life lying to literally everyone she'd ever met, Tru is kind of terrible at keeping secrets from my little sister.

"I cannot believe you two blew another date!" Sage shouts, not angry, just effusive. I call it "love yelling."

"It wasn't exactly our fault," Tru tries for the third time, but Sage holds up her hand to stop her from speaking.

We made it as far as the living room sofa before Sage extracted the first confession from Tru. All she had to do was ask how the movie was and Tru cracked, admitting that we hadn't seen more than the first two minutes. It was all downhill from there.

"Look, I appreciate how charming it is that you got my sister so hot and bothered that she tripped her security alarm, but I'm going to have to take this out of your hands for now." She spins on her heel and points at Embry and Amethyst. "You two, we need a work-around for this pulse monitor, whatever it takes. Nothing that will alert Underhill, obviously. Something temporary because we know Lila cannot stand to break the rules for too long."

"I will make an exception in cases of injustice," I offer, but I don't think Sage really cares in the moment.

"We're already working on it," Embry says.

"We only need a few more hours," Amethyst adds.

Sage turns back to face us, hands pressed together as if in prayer. "I am going to take over the logistics of your next date, okay? I'll make the reservations, get you a car, make an itinerary, I'll even pick your outfits. All you have to do"—she pauses, making intentional eye contact with both of us in turn—"is follow the plan."

"Okay, Sage," I promise, amused that out of everything we told her, the part that really stuck out was the fact that we failed a second date.

"We're lucky to have you," Tru adds.

Sage draws in a deep breath. "I know. Okay, what is it that you actually want to talk about? I can see you both have 'something' face."

As usual, I'm astounded by the speed with which my sister can pivot. Not to mention her ability to see straight through us.

"What on earth is 'something' face?" Amethyst asks.

"You know it when you see it," Embry answers.

"Obviously I don't, if they have it and I just asked what it was." Amethyst narrows his eyes at Embry.

"We want to contact Silver," I say, interrupting them before they can really get going, "and set up a meeting."

Embry clears his throat to ask, "Why, exactly?"

"Because," Tru says. "If Silver knows Logan is alive, then chances are good others do, too. I haven't been able to reach him and I'm starting to worry there's an external reason for that."

"There has to be a reason they're reaching out to Tru right now," I add. "And while all of this"—I wave the hand with the pulse monitor—"is irritating, Logan might actually be in real trouble."

I know the thought had crossed Tru's mind, but her face tightens when I say it out loud.

There's a moment of quiet while everyone digests what we've said. Then Embry raises his hand.

"I feel like someone should point out that if Logan Dire—the Ghoul of Kansas City—needs help, then the situation is, please forgive the pun, probably pretty dire and are we really the ones to do anything about it?"

"Who else is there?" Amethyst asks. "I mean, that we trust?"

Embry winces, but doesn't protest further.

"When are we doing this?" Sage asks.

"As soon as possible," Tru says. Now that she's made the decision, I can see that she's anxious and eager. "We're calling them now."

"Wait, don't we need to prepare?" Sage asks in some alarm.

"What is there to prepare?" Amethyst asks.

"I don't know! A code? A meeting point with good sight lines? An escape route in case it's a massive setup to kidnap Tru and take her far, far away?"

"That seems unlikely," Tru says. "But it's a reasonable point. I'll ask to meet outside the First Cup. It's in a residential neighborhood with quick access to main roads if we need a getaway. Does that work?"

"That works," Sage agrees, still looking less than pleased.

"Okay," Tru says, blowing out a breath. "Let's call Silver."

Silver agrees to Tru's terms and the meeting is set for 11 p.m. at the First Cup. Tru even gets Silver to agree to me coming along. Just me, though. At least officially.

The others will wait in the shadows, keeping an eye out for any signs of the kidnappers Sage hypothesized. They are already in place when Tru and I park a few blocks away and walk the rest of the way. Streetlights wash the main road and little strip of shops in sticky orange light. We cut between two houses and keep to the shadows as we get close. Across the street, a single light glows within the First Cup. They've been closed for hours, but I can still smell the earthy roast of coffee on the air.

We stop close enough to Amethyst's hiding place that he can speak without revealing himself. The others are positioned strategically so that if there's trouble, we'll have a heads-up, and so that if one of them is discovered, we'll still have two in hiding.

"Silver's people are inside those two cars on the north side of Fiftieth Street," Amethyst whispers. "Another waiting around the corner on Fifty-First and a fourth in that driveway directly across the street."

The cars parked on the street are obvious. I could have picked them out when I was ten years old because that's their purpose. They're the decoy, meant to prevent us from finding the cars that are actually surveilling us. Still, four cars for a meeting with two girls seems like overkill.

"How many inside?" Tru asks, tipping her head to get a look at the additional cars without being obvious.

"Three in the vehicles on Fiftieth, two in the one across the street, and at least two in the car on Fifty-First, but there could be more."

Seven. They brought seven people for a single conversation.

"Seems like an awful lot of security for a casual chat," I say.

"But not for a kidnapping," Amethyst suggests.

"They're moving," Tru announces as the passenger side door of one of the obvious cars opens and a figure emerges.

They step into the glow of streetlights and begin to make their way toward the coffee shop. They move with care, their steps slow and measured, their shoulders rounded forward and wrapped in a shawl despite the early summer warmth and humidity. I wait for any sign from Embry or Sage that we should abandon ship and run, but hear nothing.

"Our turn," Tru says.

Amethyst stays put while Tru and I backtrack from our position, cut through a couple yards, and emerge on the sidewalk a few doors down from where Amethyst is stationed. We keep our hands visible and carry only our phones so that anyone watching doesn't think we're armed. Which we are, because we're not fools.

Together, Tru and I jog across the street, and as the approaching figure stops beneath another streetlight, I see them more clearly—a Black woman with hair braided and twisted into a bun that covers the back of her head. When she turns, her hair flashes silver in the orange light.

The woman, who must be Silver, stops and stands with her hands clasped in front of her soft belly. "Hello, Gertrude," she says with what sounds like real admiration in her voice. "It is good to finally meet you in person. And you must be Lila Morgan," she adds, but her attention is only on me for a second before she turns back to Tru. "You really do look like your mother."

"Who are you?" Tru asks with an almost imperceptible tremor in her voice.

"My name is Anna Mirth," says Silver.

Tru shakes her head, wary but curious. "I don't know you."

"Oh, you wouldn't. I only knew your mother briefly, before you were born." There's a bittersweet note to her voice and her eyes soften. "I am so sorry for your loss."

Tru is suddenly very, very still, her breath quick and quiet.

I recognize the swift and brutal way grief asserts itself. In moments like this, years-old hurt can feel vibrant and fresh.

"What do you know about Logan?" I ask, giving Tru a moment to gather herself.

Anna Mirth takes a deep breath and lets it out slowly, bobbing her head as if resigning herself to a more contentious conversation than she was hoping for.

"I suppose I should start by telling you that I do not want to hurt Logan. In fact, I would like to help him as he once helped me. To be honest, I was hoping he would show up tonight and make this whole thing a lot easier." She laughs at herself. "But I should have known better."

"Is that why you have all that backup?" I ask, tipping my head toward the many cars waiting in the wings. "So you could have a conversation with him?"

Anna narrows her eyes at me. "So I could confirm that he's okay."

"Why wouldn't he be okay?" Tru asks.

Anna Mirth hesitates, glancing up and down the street before answering. "Because Anderson Flynn is in town."

"What does he have to do with Logan?" I ask, but Tru follows up with a more direct question: "What did Logan do?"

As soon as she's asked it, the pieces click together in my brain. There's really only one answer that explains Logan Dire's reputation.

"He killed Anderson's daughter," Anna Mirth says plainly.

"On a bounty?" Tru asks. Even if there are people who hold

a grudge against Logan, they would be bound from taking any action against him as long as he was working on an approved bounty. That's Underhill law. I can't imagine even Anderson Flynn going against something as foundational as that.

"There was a bounty," Anna confirms. "But it was a different time. Underhill was in transition. Technology was changing the way bounties were issued and claimed, and the system was easy to hack. It was even possible for kill bounties to be issued without oversight."

I've heard the stories. It's one of the reasons BountyApp exists today. And from even what little I know about how the Flynn family built their empire in the West, it's easy to believe someone would want to hurt them. And just as easy that they would go after someone for executing a bounty that was never supposed to be issued. Even if that person—even if Logan—had no way to know that.

Tru shakes her head. "Logan wouldn't have taken a kill bounty he didn't know was real."

"No?" Anna asks. "That kind of thing used to happen more than we like to remember. It was a bad time for Underhill because they couldn't punish people for acting in good faith. Not even Enforcers. Not even when people were killed. And the strange truth is that the system was working better than anything that had come before it." Anna takes a breath before adding, "But Anderson's daughter was only twelve years old."

Tru's mouth falls open, but no sound comes out.

I feel a softer echo of her shock. Not from years of knowing Logan, but from knowing Tru. Yes, Logan killed people and, yes, he taught Tru to do the same. But killing children isn't the kind of thing that just goes away.

"Why haven't we heard about this?" I ask, resisting the urge to reach for Tru's hand. Resisting the urge to think about my own father.

Anna sighs. "It is how he came to be known as the Ghoul."

"There had to have been a mistake," Tru whispers.

"Anderson has held a grudge ever since, but Logan was more or less untouchable and then"—Anna holds up her hands—"he disappeared. Now he's back and within reach. I'm afraid Anderson Flynn isn't going to give up the chance to seek revenge."

"So Logan *is* in danger?" Tru steps forward, voice climbing with panic. Anna takes a startled step back before throwing out a hand to stop her not-so-hidden guard from coming to her rescue.

"I believe he is. I reached out to you so that you could warn him. Get a message to him and tell him to get out of town while he still can," she adds.

"And even if she could warn him, then what?" I demand. "Where should he go? Underhill's hold on talents gets weaker the farther you get from Kansas City, and the West is Flynn territory. Even with Anderson Flynn here, it's probably safer for Logan to also be here. Why are you coming to us, instead of telling Underhill about a threat right under their noses?"

"Because I have no proof," she answers smoothly, but there's an edge to her now that wasn't there before. The sharp corner of a secret I didn't notice earlier.

"What if something has already happened to him and no one knows?" Tru asks, balling her fists at her sides. "Please come with us to Underhill and speak with Boss Acosta. Even if you don't have proof."

Anna's demeanor shifts. She glances nervously down the street. A quiet echo of nerves skitters down my spine. Because Anna has at least five guards within shouting distance and she's still worried.

"I have to go," Anna says. "I've said enough."

"You've hardly said anything at all!" Tru protests.

At this Anna frowns. "I'm sorry, I can't. I don't tangle with the Flynns."

"But you reached out to me!" Tru nearly shouts. "If you weren't willing to tangle with the Flynns, why do anything at all?"

Anna twists her hands before her, seeming to consider her words carefully.

"Logan and your mother saved my life once. I wanted to repay the debt if I could," she says plainly. "I'm very sorry, but I—I can't help you now. I can't get involved. The most I can do is tell you to be very, *very* careful."

She starts to back away and I scramble for something, anything, to say that might make her stay. Give us something.

"We'll go to Boss Acosta!" I say, hoping I'm right and this is something she wants to avoid, that avoiding Underhill and Embry's mother is why she's taken steps to protect her identity, why her nervousness ratcheted up when we suggested turning to them. "We'll tell her everything we know about you."

Anna pauses long enough to offer a pitying smile. "I'm nobody. And Underhill isn't interested in making enemies with the Flynns any more than I am."

And without another word, she turns on her heel and hurries back to her car.

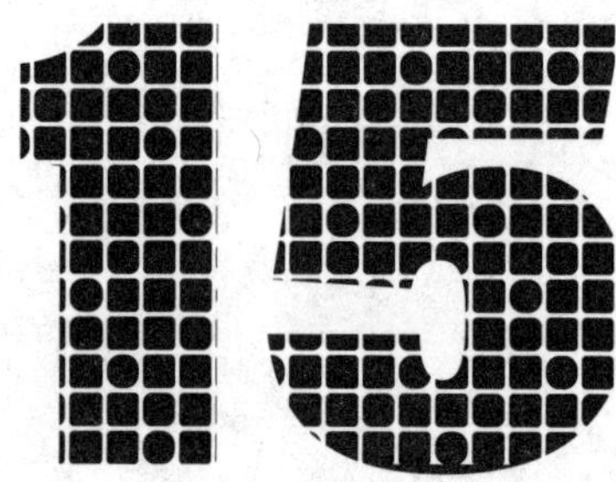

Back at home, Tru stress-preps a batch of croissants, and I keep her company while the rest of Sage's intrepid gang gathers around the kitchen table and searches for every scrap of information they can find on the Flynns—or Anna Mirth, but it seems she wasn't kidding when she claimed to be nobody. The Flynns keep a low profile; Anna Mirth may as well not exist.

Watching Tru work, I realize that I've never really appreciated the complexity of a croissant. At the same time, it's surprisingly simple and straightforward. She builds a base layer of flour, water, and half-and-half, folds in a thick layer of butter, and then folds that over and over again before sealing the dough in plastic wrap and popping it in the fridge. She explains that she'll repeat the folding process for days until the dough is fully laminated. I can't help thinking that people are made the same way—base layers that gain complexity, texture, and history with every year that passes.

"Okay," Sage announces, standing up with Amethyst's pad of paper in her hand. "This is what we know so far: Anderson Flynn owns two casinos in Vegas, has a distant family relation here in Kansas City, and otherwise seems to do his best to stay out of the public eye. There's a record of Anderson's daughter's death that tracks with Anna's story. She was twelve years old, her name was Simone, and the funeral was held here in Kansas City. But we haven't found anything that links them—at least overtly—to Logan Dire or the Ghoul of Kansas City, which is probably because that kind of thing would be recorded on something like micro fish."

"Micro*fiche*," Amethyst corrects, with a small smile on his lips.

"That's what I said," Sage agrees.

Amethyst looks over at Embry. "Maybe we should just go to your mom," he says, dropping his phone to the table with a thud. "We tell her that we have reason to believe that regardless of why he told her he was here, Mr. Flynn is seeking revenge for his daughter. And we see what she says."

Embry lowers his own phone and nods thoughtfully. "Okay, she's going to ask us for proof, which we don't have. All we have is hearsay, and my mom won't give it a second thought."

"It wouldn't be hearsay if Anna Mirth would just nut up and come forward," Sage says quickly.

"We still wouldn't have proof," I say. "She's made a highly educated guess."

"And I hate to be the downer here, but I think it's safe to assume that my mom knows as much about Logan's history as Anna does and has made the same guess." Embry frowns in distaste before adding, "She's just choosing not to do anything about it because of politics."

"We need help," Tru whispers.

I reach for her hand and squeeze. I can guess what she's thinking—Logan is the person she would turn to for help and he's not here.

He's a question mark and he has been since the night he texted to let her know he was alive.

My father isn't here, but at least I know he's not coming back. I know no one can hurt him anymore, and it's strange to find that there's a twisted degree of comfort in that.

"I wish—" Tru starts, then cuts herself off.

"Do you think he really killed her?" Sage asks softly.

"I think there has to be another explanation," Tru answers quickly.

We don't say anything because there's nothing to say. Logan's history speaks for itself. Even if he isn't guilty of this, he has probably done things that we would all find difficult to defend.

"Do you?" Tru asks with a hint of alarm.

It's Sage who speaks up first. "He was one of the most terrifying enforcers in Underhill history, Tru," she says, pointedly not answering the question.

"But you all knew him," Tru says.

"We knew Papa Stallard. We also grew up hearing ghost stories about the Ghoul," Amethyst offers apologetically.

Embry leans forward to rest his elbows on his knees. He says, "Sometimes people surprise you in the worst ways."

"Lila?" Tru asks, turning the full force of her mosaic eyes on me.

There's a surge in my chest, a sudden swelling of tissue and organs that feels like I'm dying. In my head, I know I'm not. It's a physiological response to extreme emotion, but it hurts just the same.

My own father did so much to resist who he was. In the end, it didn't matter and that's all that people remember.

But I remember. He was more than his final moment, and Logan was more than his early moments. Whatever those may have been.

"People change," I say. "Maybe having you changed him."

Tru thinks quietly for a moment.

"I don't think that's the answer," she says, voice soft without being small. "All I can think of is how it felt to knock on his door when I was ten. How terrifying it was when he opened the door with a knife in hand, but how even in that moment I knew that he wouldn't hurt me. Not even if his life depended on it."

She looks up at us, and even though there's a glimmer of tears in her eyes, there's no shame and no doubt.

"I've known since he opened that door that he was a killer with principles. It's the only reason I'm alive today. He never would have killed a child," she says. "Having me did change him. But not like that."

"Then," Amethyst starts and pauses, his usually unbothered expression dipping toward an uncomfortable amount of sympathy. He clears his throat and starts again. "Then, why isn't he here?"

Tru looks down at her phone. "I don't know," she says, and then. "Maybe he's angry with me."

I remember what she said at the movie theater about joining Underhill, about him seeing that as something she'd done wrong. This seems deeper than that. "Why would he be angry with you?" I ask.

"Because." Tru swallows, biting back tears. "He changed everything about his own life to support mine, made sure that I knew how to live without exposing my true talent to the world, and at the first opportunity, that's exactly what I did. I chose to be seen and to live in the open despite the risks. Everyone knows who and what I am, and that means all his work was for nothing. Of course he would be angry with me." She shrugs a little helplessly and for the first time I see the holes in her armor. "Why else would Logan stay away at a moment like this? He's not here because he doesn't *want* to be."

"Or maybe he took the long overdue opportunity to go to Disney World or something and we're all stressing for nothing," Embry says in an attempt to lighten the mood.

"Maybe I should just go straight to Anderson Flynn and ask him if—" Tru starts, but Amethyst cuts her off.

"No way. Being a bastion doesn't make you invincible, and one of the few other things we know about Anderson Flynn is that he has an unhealthy obsession with bastions," he says. "There is no way to convince us that you wouldn't be walking into the proverbial lion's den, so if that's your current argument, save it."

Tru closes her mouth.

"Just so we're all clear, we need a plan that *doesn't* involve potential sacrifice," Sage says with a pointed look in Tru's direction. "Okay?"

"So, what do you suggest?" I ask.

Sage frowns at nothing, the way she always has when she's thinking. "Well," she says after a long moment. "We clearly need to do some reconnaissance."

"I can help with that," Embry volunteers, but Sage shakes her head.

"Have you already forgotten that your skills are needed elsewhere?" She arches her eyebrows, waiting for him to recall what he's forgotten. "Lila's pulse monitor!"

"Right, but . . . isn't this a little more important than that?" he asks, then turns to me with an apologetic smile.

"Hardly," Sage answers with a scoff, not giving me a chance to respond. "Besides, Lila and Tru are most suited for this job. And it's perfect because while they're doing that, you and Amethyst can crack her monitor, and I can plan their date."

She tops this declaration off with a beaming smile.

"Sage," I say. "I hate to agree with Embry, but I do think

there are more important things to focus on right now than a date."

"You can always plan a date for us later," Tru adds, a faint blush creeping into her cheeks when she meets my eyes.

"Oh, Lila. Oh, Tru," Sage says, patting our heads like we're silly cats. "Sometimes, when things get really stressful and strange, the best thing we can do is continue to live our lives the way we want to. And that's what you two are going to do. Even if I have to drag you to the restaurant myself."

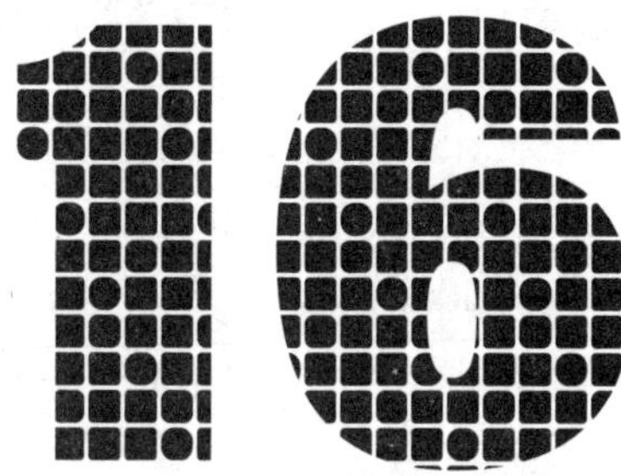

I have to hand it to my little sister: She knows how to plan a date.

Following Sage's very detailed instructions, we take Tru's car and park it in the public lot near Union Station before hopping on the streetcar and riding it to the stop near the Kauffman Center.

"At the end of your date, you'll take the streetcar up to the River Market and get a tasty, tasty ice cream dessert at Betty Rae's," Sage had instructed as she reviewed the itinerary with me. "Tru really loves mint chocolate chip. That's free advice from me to you, but it's your job to make sure she gets it, okay?"

"Okay," I'd said, doing my best not to think about how this date was going to stress my eternally stressed bank account. But just as I had the thought, Sage hit me with a beaming smile and said, "By the way, I've called ahead and taken care of all the charges, so you can stop doing that private fretting you've been doing and just enjoy yourself."

I opened my mouth to protest but she was ready for me.

"My plan, my payment options," she said with a shrug. "I don't make the rules; I just abide by them. Also, it's not my card. It's Embry's and he insists," she said in a way that I suspect means she was insisting on his behalf. "Plus, there's nothing you can do about it now."

"This is not normal," I'd said. Softly, because I was having trouble breathing through how it felt to have so much support from my sister and her friends.

"This was never going to be normal, but not because I'm making it happen," Sage said with another shrug. "If this were a normal date, we wouldn't be hacking into a police-state monitoring device so you can get a little worked up without calling out the guard. If this were a normal date, I wouldn't be double-checking that both you and Tru are armed and wearing shoes you can run in. If this were a normal date—"

"I get this point," I'd said, holding up a hand.

"Great," she answered with a smile. "So, let's just lean into it being something else. Do you want to review the itinerary one more time?"

She was right, of course. This was never going to be a normal date, as I'm reminded when both Tru and I clock the exits the second we enter the restaurant. This was always going to be something else. Something unique to who I am and who Tru is, and I think Sage is right. That's okay.

As the hostess hands us our menus and promises that our server will be right with us, I pull out my cell phone and text Sage that we've arrived at the little wine bar she selected for us and all is well.

"Do you think Sage realizes that we're not old enough to order any wine in the wine bar?" Tru asks, lips twisting in amusement.

"She does, but she didn't send us here for the wine," I say, glad that Sage prepared me for this. "Amethyst says this place has the best French fries in the city."

"Who am I to question Amethyst's tastes?" Tru says. "I really like fries," she adds. "Logan was deeply, profoundly against fried foods, so I only ever have them on special occasions. And I think this counts."

She smiles, but I can tell that she's nervous.

I probably should be, too. This is our third attempt at a date. The stakes feel higher than ever. But I feel calm just being with her.

"It counts," I say, and I reach across the table to take her hand in mine.

Something glints between us, and our eyes fall to the black band encircling my wrist. Tru's thumb grazes over mine and it's whisper soft, but I feel the echo of it flutter down my spine. My heartbeat quickens, my entire body seeming to respond to that single touch, and I do my best to slow my breath and silently thank Embry and Amethyst for finding a way to deactivate it. Even if it's just for tonight.

"I wish I could do something about this," she says, thumb

skimming over mine once more. "And I wish I could say that it's temporary and will get better."

I know she's talking about the monitor and Underhill, but all I can think about right now is the frisson of electricity between our skin and how much more I'd like to feel.

"Yeah," I murmur as my heart races.

Luckily, the server chooses that moment to come to our table. Tru releases my hand and the simmering, sweet tension inside me begins to ease. By the time I plug back into the conversation, the server is suggesting that we start with two orders of pommes frites instead of one—because chances are good that we'll want more—and goes on to list our drink options. I ask Tru to pick for both of us and, with fries and drinks taken care of, we turn our full attention to the menu.

I glance down the list of entrées and find that in addition to the usual steak, chicken, and pork offerings, there are two kinds of fish on the menu.

"I haven't had much fish in my life, but it always sounds interesting," I say. "I'm also afraid to order it because what if I hate it? It's so expensive."

"We could share the pan-seared snapper and get the hamburger as a backup," Tru suggests.

She says it casually, but the idea of sharing food with her stirs a new kind of excitement in me. There's something unabashedly intimate about sharing a plate. Even if we split it before we've taken a single bite.

"That sounds nice," I say weakly, and Tru nods with conviction. Decision made.

Our server returns with our drinks and two baskets of perfectly golden pommes frites. We order the snapper and the burger before they zip away again, then we dig into fries that are every bit as delicious as promised.

"So," I say, partly to force myself to breathe between bites. "How did you convince Logan to train you? I mean, is it okay if I ask about him?"

There's a split second of hesitation before Tru answers. "He didn't want to. I think he worried that if I could do what he did, I'd spend my whole life living for revenge. And he wasn't wrong, but I think he also realized that I was going to do that anyway. But really, I just asked him. Repeatedly. Until he said yes." Her expression softens, a memory I'm not privy to stealing her thoughts for a second. "Baking was part of the deal, though."

"How so?" I ask. "So you could always carb up before a workout?"

"No, although that was a definite perk. He said I needed a hobby that wasn't intended for violence. I could pick anything I wanted."

"Why'd you pick baking?"

"Because," she starts and stops, swallowing as though pained. When she speaks again, her voice is tight. "Because it made me think of my parents, and because—because it was what Logan did, and that made me feel safe."

I catch an echo of her pain in my own chest, and my throat squeezes tight against memories that are as different as they are similar.

"Leave it to Logan to turn baking into a full-body sport, though. I always feel like I'm doing the recipe wrong when I skip the weighted vest. Do you have something like that?" she asks in an almost whisper. "Something that makes you think of your parents."

The question catches me off guard, which is ridiculous since I started this far too serious conversation. I don't remember the last time someone asked me a question about my parents that wasn't loaded with judgment. I breathe carefully for a moment before answering.

"My dad used to meditate. He would go out in the backyard and sit beneath the big maple tree. It always seemed like he was there for hours. Sometimes my mom would join him and sometimes we would all do it together. When my talent emerged, he taught me to use meditation to clear my mind and learn control. I think a lot of bombshells do similar things. Ms. Jones used to count when she felt her control slipping. One to a hundred over and over again." I shrug and drop my gaze to the basket of fries. "Dad stopped meditating after mom died."

"But you didn't?" Tru asks.

"It took me a while to realize I didn't need him to do it on my own," I say. "But it helps and it reminds me of when things were good with us. When we were all happy."

Tru reaches for my hand and squeezes. Talking like this, it's easy to see all the parallels in our lives—our parents are dead, our adoptive guardians gone, our talents regarded with suspicion or mistrust—it makes me feel less alone.

It feels good, and that makes me want to share more than I ever have before.

"It took me so long to feel even remotely secure again after my father died," I say, ignoring the warm press of tears in my eyes. "I tried to do everything right and now—" I stop.

"You didn't do anything wrong," Tru says with a tremble of anger in her voice. For me, I realize. "They're just afraid and when people are afraid, they do stupid things."

"I know," I say, and now it's Ryan's voice in my mind. Telling me that Underhill will never let me grow to my full potential.

Our food arrives and we learn that while I love pan-seared snapper, Tru strongly prefers the burger. We also end up with a third helping of pommes frites because it didn't occur to us that more would come with the burger, but this isn't a problem. We laugh and eat, and just as Sage promised, the bill is completely covered at the end.

We leave and hop back on the streetcar, taking it to the River Market for dessert per Sage's instructions.

"What if we took a little walk first?" Tru suggests.

"You mean, before ice cream? You want to deviate from Sage's well-designed, carefully curated plan?" I ask in mock horror.

Tru leans in close, winding her fingers through mine as she tips her mouth toward my ear and whispers, "I do."

I can't actually describe what the heat of her breath against my neck does to me. Only that I am liquid and stone-solid all at once. Only that my insides shiver and melt. Only that I want nothing more than to follow this girl away from the bright lights of the ice cream parlor so that the shadows will give us a sliver of privacy.

Only that I want to kiss her. More than I ever have before.

Without another word, I let her pull me toward a dark corner and into the narrow alley beyond.

And that, apparently, is our mistake.

We have only taken a few steps when I feel the shadows closing in at our backs. An alarm hums in my mind as two figures step into the alley behind us, blocking the already faint light of the main street.

"Lila," Tru whispers, her hand tightening in mine.

"I know," I say, securing my grip on hers. "Keep walking."

I know this neighborhood but not well. There are apartment complexes and new restaurants everywhere. If it were the weekend, this area would be thick with nightlife, but it's not the weekend and the streets bear only a few locals hurrying home.

I angle my steps toward the riverfront and Tru follows suit, but as soon as we turn the corner, another figure steps into our path, blocking our way forward.

A quick glance over my shoulder confirms there's only one behind us now. Making this one a wingtip.

They're both dressed in dark clothes and soft running shoes, faces blurred behind scrubbers. The combination is a really bad sign.

"Which one of you is the bombshell?"

Tru tenses at my side as a bright anger burns in my chest. It seems the council's "protective measures" have given some people the excuse they needed to weaponize their fear and come after bombshells themselves.

Great.

Tru steps forward, still holding on to my hand. "I am," she says.

It takes me a second to understand what she's done. And before I can correct her, I'm hit from behind.

Pain explodes in my head. I hear Tru call my name and then gasp. I press one hand to my head, willing my vision to clear so I can fight back. But a hand clamps a cloth over my mouth and nose. I smell the sharp, floral notes of lavender, combined with something acrid and chemical. And then nothing.

The Fourth Explosion of Lila Morgan

I knew my father's accident would have ripple effects for the rest of my life. I just didn't expect that the people I'd once considered friends would be so quick to turn on me.

By the time I went back to St. Isidor's, there was a petition in place to have me removed from the building for the foreseeable future. Parents were angry and scared and absolutely positive that it wasn't a question of if I lost control of myself, but when. I wasn't exactly in the right state of mind to prove them wrong, which could have led to disaster if Ms. Jones hadn't made me her mission.

She arrived at the school as I sat in the principal's office, unsure if I was about to be suspended for something I hadn't done yet. Ms. Jones swept in with the kind of authority that made the entire office go quiet. Then, ignoring everyone else, she introduced herself to me as Underhill, Inc.'s chief of Ops.

"I'm also a bombshell," she said. "Did you know that?"

I nodded. She was the most famous bombshell in Underhill.

Or, she had been until my father lost control and killed a dozen innocent people.

"All these people think they know you. They think they know who you are and what you'll do, but I think they're wrong," she said, looking hard into my eyes. She looked stately and sharp in Operations blue, her hair pulled into a severe bun, and her lips painted deep red. "Do you want to prove them all wrong, Lila Morgan?" she asked.

"Yes," I'd answered. I'd never wanted anything more.

"Are you ready to work harder than you ever have before?"

"Yes," I'd answered again.

"Good." She turned back to the principal and raised her voice so anyone near could hear every word. "Lila Morgan is my protégé. I expect any issues with her and her talent will be brought to my attention immediately, and I expect her to receive the same consideration all students receive at St. Isidor's."

She didn't wait for a response of any kind because it wasn't a question.

"Lila, I'll see you tomorrow after school. Report to Underhill and Mr. Bern will tell you where to go."

"Yes, ma'am," I said.

And that was that. My training started the very next day. Every day after school, I went to Underhill and spent hours by her side, learning and practicing. And I didn't hear anything more about anyone trying to get me kicked out of school.

But that was because they'd merely changed their approach. Instead of going after me directly, they went after the one person that I cared about more than anyone in the world.

I was practicing with Ms. Jones when it happened. Near the end of our session, I got a text message from a number I didn't know. A video of Sage with tears in her eyes, firelight reflecting there.

"One second for every life," said the person holding the phone.

Sage gritted her teeth in the video and before I could comprehend what was happening, she stepped forward and placed her hand into the open flames.

I knew she screamed, but I didn't hear it. I heard nothing but my own fury as my talent erupted with full force.

A distant part of my mind understood that it was precisely what her torturers wanted, but it was a whisper compared to the part of me that wanted to lash out.

When I returned to consciousness, Ms. Jones was still there. She placed a bottle of water on the floor next to me and pillowed my head on my abandoned sweatshirt, and she sat on a chair she pulled from the edge of the practice room. She watched me with an expression of compassionate disappointment.

"That was not ideal," she said.

"I have to go," I said, pushing onto my hands and knees. "Sage—"

"She'll be fine," Ms. Jones interrupted. "And those children with her will all see the consequences of their actions. Sit. Rest and drink your water. In five minutes, we're going to practice again."

I started to refuse. I was exhausted and that was the worst time to even think about using my talent, but Ms. Jones raised a finger, warding off my protest with the simple motion.

"Not your talent," she said. "We're going to work on your emotions. They are as volatile as your talent right now, but they do not have to be. By the time we're through, you won't just be able to control your talent; you'll be able to control your heart, too. And when you can do that, no one will ever be able to hurt you again."

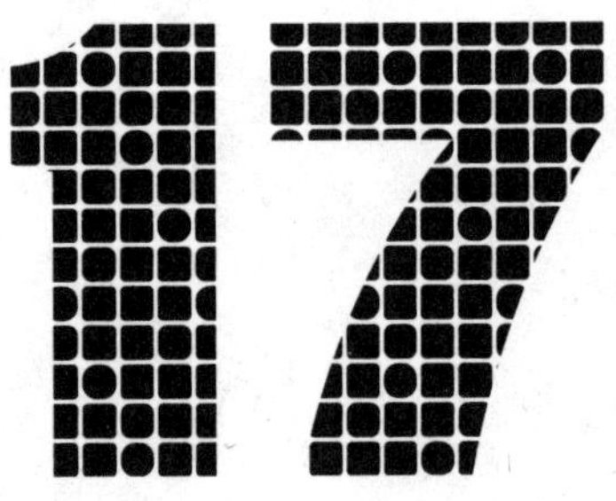

I wake to darkness, the chirping of birds, and a throbbing headache. A surge of unease rockets through me, followed by a wave of nausea. The latter wins and I roll to one side and vomit up the complete contents of my stomach.

Bile burns at the back of my throat, and I hear the splatter of sick against a hard floor, but the thing that bothers me most are the bands of steel around each wrist. Handcuffs, and the reason I can't see is that there's a black-out mask covering my eyes.

All at once, I remember the attack and a blur of movement and pain before someone shook me awake and—

Tru. I remember her voice. The frantic sound of it asking if I was all right, but she sounded far away. No, not far away. She was on a phone. Whoever grabbed me called her to prove that I was alive.

I remember trying to tell her anything I could, and then nothing. The pain in my head suggests they knocked me out—twice?—and the vomit on the floor suggests at least a minor concussion. The bastards.

I squeeze my eyes against the pain and try to remember even more about that night. I remember walking with Tru after dinner and being attacked on the road. I remember them asking which of us was the bombshell and Tru defending me without a beat of hesitation. I remember the scent of lavender.

And then they grabbed me. Except they thought I was her. Which means . . . they grabbed the wrong person.

I go still and quiet, listening to my surroundings. I hear voices beyond a door that seem to come close and then drift away again, the distance and muffled sounds of traffic, and the sound I had taken for the chirping of birds is actually the very recognizable beeping of hospital monitors. Once I've placed the sound, I recognize the sterile, bleach-riddled scent in the air, but before I can open my mouth to call out for help, I notice something else: the very quiet inhale and exhale of breath.

There is someone else in this room with me.

"Who are you?" I ask.

No answer. Instead, I hear the rustle of fabric as someone stands and I brace for an attack I'll never see coming.

But the footsteps don't come for me. They angle away and I hear the soft sweep of a door opening, the torrent of sound from outside pouring in before it shuts again.

This would be my moment to scream for help. But if my captors are confident enough to leave the room without gagging me, the chance that screaming will do one lick of good seems insignificant.

It's only a second before the door opens again. This time, I hear two sets of footsteps enter the room.

"You're awake. That's good. It's about time we had a chat."

The mask is pulled from my eyes, and I blink at the sudden light. As expected, I'm in a hospital room—or something that looks like one—handcuffed to a hospital bed. I'm still dressed in the same clothing I wore on my date, but my boots are gone, and there are two men I don't recognize standing on either side of the bed. One is younger and poised so that he might easily reach for a weapon should the very intimidating girl strapped to a bed make a sudden move, and the other is Anderson Flynn. He is standing on the side of the bed I didn't puke on.

"Good morning, Lila. My name is Anderson Flynn." He pauses as if he expects a dramatic reaction, but when I don't give him the pleasure, he continues. "I won't insult your intelligence by pretending we meant to grab you instead of your friend—"

"Girl," I interrupt.

"Excuse me?" he asks in genuine surprise.

"Girlfriend," I say, careful to enunciate the word.

A flash of irritation narrows his eyes. "Instead of Ms. Grey," he finishes, seemingly unwilling to say the word, but then he stops, nods to himself, and tries again. "I mean, your girlfriend. I wanted to apologize for the mistake and for your injury."

He stops again, eyes on me, and I have the distinct impression that he's waiting for me to say something.

"What do you want with her?" I ask finally.

"Nothing," he answers.

"I thought we weren't insulting my intelligence," I say.

He laughs, a gentle, grandfatherly chuckle engineered to put me off my guard. "Indeed. All right, yes, we did want something from her, but it seems that we can accomplish that same goal with you. We don't need you to do anything except stay here for a few more days. If you can do that, no further harm will come to you, and if all goes well, this won't take very long."

"If what goes well?" I ask.

"Just a simple transaction," he answers without answering at all.

I hold his gaze, daring him to answer me. Even without taking into account what we learned from Silver—from Anna Mirth—there's only one reason I can think of that anyone would want Tru, who, before a few months ago, was known to exactly no one in Underhill.

"You want Logan Dire," I say.

"Ah!" he says with a pleased smile. "Here I am insulting your intelligence again. Forgive me. Yes, I want Logan Dire, though it is more accurate to say that I want what he can give me and Mr. Dire requires motivation."

"Tru," I say. "You want to use her to lure Logan out, so you're going to use me to lure her out."

"I am," he confirms.

My stomach pitches. Tru will absolutely do something supremely ill-conceived to get me out.

"No." I'm already reaching for my song, pulling the thread of melody close, and starting to turn up the volume. If Ryan can spot-weld a fence without damaging anything else, I can break out of these restraints and get out of here.

Or not. The song swells, growing too fast. So fast that I'm suddenly out of breath.

"Ah, I wouldn't do that, if I were you," Anderson says, raising a condescending eyebrow and gesturing to our surroundings. "We are inside a real hospital room."

"And?" I gasp, sweat beading along my forehead. My head aches where they hit me and nausea roils in my stomach, the concussion symptoms making the song resonating through me almost too much to bear. I may not be able to melt through my handcuffs, but I have enough control to make this explosion a small one. If the only other person I injure is Anderson Flynn, I can live with that.

"I'm glad you asked. You see, we're in a very special, very secure ward of the hospital. If you were to lose control, even a little bit, you might end up murdering several very innocent, very young lives."

At that, the other man in the room crosses to the door and pops it open. Not all the way, but enough that I can hear the sounds: monitors beeping, the mechanical press of hand sanitizer stations as nurses enter and leave patient rooms, and the cry of babies. So thin and small. So *new*.

My mouth goes dry; my song instantly dies.

"I thought that would be the case," Anderson says as the other man lets the door shut. "I have heard about you, Lila Morgan. You've got potential, but you're still learning. Still trying to figure out what kind of talent you want to be. Or maybe it's that you're trying to decide between being the kind of talent Underhill wants you to be or being yourself."

I know he's trying to draw me in, to manipulate me into asking him for something.

But half the battle is knowing the field we're fighting on, and right now I don't know much at all.

So I give him an inch.

"How would you know that?" I ask.

I know I've asked the right question by the way his smile grows. "Insulting *my* intelligence now, are we? We have a mutual acquaintance. He thinks highly of you."

I didn't catch a signal, but the door swings open once more. I know who it will be before he steps into the room, but I want to be wrong so badly that my vision blurs and I don't see him at first.

But there's no denying his voice when he says, "Hey, Lila."

"Ryan." The name is ash on my tongue.

"He has nothing but good things to say about you." Anderson pushes on as though we're all old friends. "In fact, we were planning on approaching you after all of this is settled. It's always a shame to see good talent going to waste, and when it comes to bombshells, Underhill has always excelled at letting promising young things wither on the vine."

I resist the urge to tell him that I'm not a fruit or a flower, because I have zero investment in what he thinks of me beyond current circumstances. I don't bother trying to resist the urge to get a dig in. "Maybe if you were better at recognizing talent, you wouldn't have grabbed the wrong person."

Anderson's eyes narrow on me, real anger flashing behind them for just an instant before he regains control.

"That is a fair point," he says. "But here we are, and since we are here, I'd like to make you an offer."

He pauses, perhaps expecting me to respond in some way, which I don't. We both know I have no power in this situation. Anything I say will highlight my vulnerability or sound delusional. So I wait.

He clears his throat before continuing. "I'd like you to consider working for me."

Even though I knew it was coming, it still feels absurd. "Why?" I ask.

"Because I like people who can think for themselves, and I think you'd thrive outside of Underhill. Working in the private sector, if you will. You can help us get what we want and minimize the chances that anyone you care for gets hurt."

"I'm not interested."

I may not know much about Anderson Flynn, but I know that "private sector" is just a nice way of saying "black market."

"You should give it some thought," he almost croons. "Your future with Underhill is looking highly regulated."

His pointed gaze shifts to the table by my bedside, where a familiar black band sits. My guts clench around the realization that if it hadn't been deactivated for my date, all of Underhill would likely know where I am right now. Judging by the oily smile on Anderson Flynn's face, he knows it, too.

"If you come work for me," he continues, "who can say how far you'll go?"

"Or how many people I'd kidnap?" I ask. "Or murder?"

"If you stay with Underhill, how many capture bounties would you execute? Kill bounties?" he counters smoothly. "They're the same actions, codified in a way the undiscerning find more palatable."

He holds on to his smile and he doesn't come any closer, but the threat of him is as real as a knife to my throat. He is pretending to be impressed by me, but I know that I am only the means to an end for him. A weapon he wants to hone for his own purposes.

"I'm not interested," I repeat.

Ryan shifts in my peripheral vision, hands clenching and unclenching reflexively.

Anderson Flynn's eyes dart in Ryan's direction without making contact, but still he smiles. "I thought that might be the case."

I have the distinct and dread-filled feeling that I have not only done what he expected me to, but what he wanted me to. It's the same feeling I used to get in school when I couldn't resist the taunting anymore and lashed out only to see a triumphant smile on the face of my tormentor. Bombshells can't help but go off, after all. In this case, though, I fear that I haven't just proved a point, but I've made things easier for Anderson Flynn. Cleaner somehow if he doesn't have to worry about where my loyalties do and don't lie.

"In that case, sit tight, Lila," Anderson Flynn says. "And try to relax. This will all be over soon."

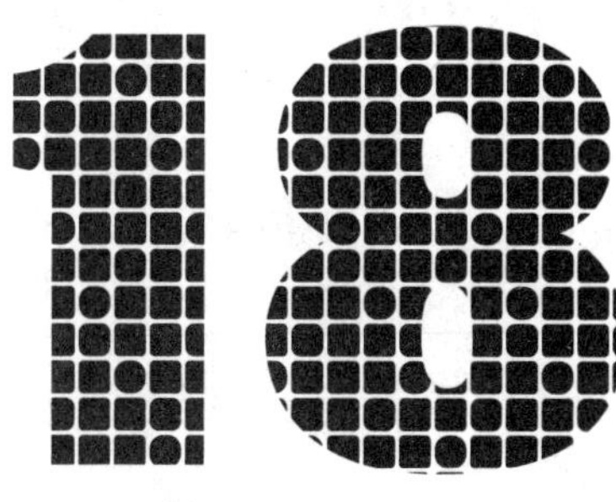

Sitting tight is not my strong suit.

Time passes with unrelenting apathy. I can almost feel every second as it ticks past, thousands of tiny cuts on my skin.

There is a TV on the wall but it's turned off and I don't see a controller anywhere. And I can't bring myself to ask these people for anything, not even a change of clothes, so I spend the time trying not to imagine all the things Tru and Sage and Amethyst and even Embry might be doing right now. All the foolish ways they might be planning to get me out.

A quiet, terrified part of me worries that they won't try.

There is a guard in the room and I'm certain another outside the door. They rotate on a schedule that feels regular even if I can't accurately gauge the hours between each. The casual way in which they come and go suggests that if Mr. Flynn doesn't outright own this entire hospital, he owns enough of the people in it to ensure he has complete privacy.

I track the passage of light outside the heavy shades on the windows. An actual nurse, as far as I can tell, comes into the room three times a day to help me to the bathroom and watch me while I eat plates of rubbery eggs or tough chicken. She doesn't say much, but the fact that she's unbothered by my hostage situation tells me everything I need to know about her. She, like who knows how many others, is in Mr. Flynn's pocket. Part of me wonders if she's here voluntarily or if she, too, is under some kind of duress. I'm not sure which option is better.

I've been here nearly three days by the time Ryan appears in my doorway again, excusing the guard with a nod of his head.

The guard doesn't hesitate, which tells me that Ryan is more senior than I would have guessed based on age alone.

"I'm so glad you've come," I say with mock civility. "I haven't had a chance to thank you for my lovely accommodations." I give my wrists a little tug. The handcuffs clatter against the sturdy plastic of the bedframe.

His eyes flick briefly to my wrists. "I'm sorry about this. It wasn't supposed to go this way."

"Right, it was supposed to be my girlfriend tied to a bed. That would have been so much better."

"I know you won't believe me, but it would have been," he answers, crossing the room to stand at my bedside. "Quicker, anyway."

"What do you want now?" I ask. "I assume you didn't actually come here to apologize."

"I wouldn't dare." He pushes one hand through his blond curls, letting the knotwork tattoos around his forearms peek out from the sleeves of his lightweight Henley. A slight blush makes him appear boyish and charming in a way I have to actively combat. "I came to tell you that it's going to happen today."

"What is?" I ask, suddenly alert.

"Your rescue attempt," he says plainly. "Well, your rescue. I shouldn't say 'attempt' when it will almost certainly be successful. Later this evening, you will be free."

The only reason he would tell me this is because he wants something from me. And I can only think of one thing he would want from me.

"I won't help you catch her," I say.

The smile he gives me is more a wince. He watches me with an expression bordering on regret, holding back whatever his boss wants him to say next. I appreciate that he doesn't say something meaningless about only being a messenger. Even now there are things I like about him.

It's supremely irritating.

"I won't," I repeat when he's been quiet for too long.

"I don't mean to sound like an asshole, but I think you will," he says.

I glare, knowing what comes next, but unwilling to make this any easier for him.

He sighs, then presses his lips together as he studies me. Choosing his next words or his next line of attack.

"You really should consider Mr. Flynn's offer," he says.

"His offer? You mean to come work for a notorious crime lord who most certainly does terrible things to good people?" I almost laugh. "There's nothing to consider."

"You think Underhill never does bad things to good people?" he asks, the disbelief in his voice rich enough to communicate he won't believe me even if I try to deny it.

"I think they try not to, which matters to me."

"Sure," he says, bobbing his head in something like acceptance. "But they are actively hurting *you*, Lila. They're restraining and constraining you, suppressing your talent instead of encouraging it. It's the exact opposite of what they're supposed to do, and the opposite of how you would be treated if you worked for Mr. Flynn."

I raise one wrist and give my handcuffs a tug. "What do you call this, then?"

"Temporary," he answers with an ironic smile. "And necessary, but not enough to hold you for any real length of time."

"It's not doing much to convince me working for Anderson Flynn will be any better than Underhill," I say. "What happens the next time I do something he doesn't like or agree with? Do the handcuffs come back out? Or do I just disappear?"

Ryan doesn't answer right away. He watches me with a thoughtful expression, his eyes boring into mine. I think he's probably searching for something, but whatever it is, I can't give it to him.

When he speaks again, his voice is low and serious.

"You're disappearing already, Lila. You just haven't realized it yet."

The words sink into me as swiftly as a blade. I nearly gasp at the pain of their impact.

He's right. He's right and I didn't see it until now. But for two months, I've been doing everything in my power to be still. Be quiet. Be good and perfect and above reproach. I've only taken up the spaces I was given, and instead of standing up for myself when I was criticized anyway, I've let others do it for me.

It was so easy to let it happen that I didn't even notice.

And the smaller I make myself, the smaller they want to make me.

Ryan's mouth pinches in a sympathetic smile. "I hope you won't let them take everything away from you, and I hope you'll consider Mr. Flynn's offer seriously."

"Oh, I'm taking it seriously," I say, but my voice lacks the strength it had a moment ago. My mind reels and nausea stirs in my gut, but I swallow hard. If Ryan sees he's gained ground, he'll keep pushing. "And I'm still not going to help you kidnap my girlfriend."

He sighs, raising his phone to show me a picture of Sage seated on the sofa of Tru's house. She's not looking at the camera, which means she didn't know the picture was being taken; Sage rarely misses an opportunity to choose her angle. Whoever took this did so without Sage knowing.

"Who took this?" I ask, afraid that I already know the answer.

"I did," he says. "When I visited them to share what I know about where you're being held."

My heart hammers against my chest, pulsing in the artery at my neck so hard I'm sure Ryan can see it.

"They were suspicious at first, so don't be too upset with them," Ryan says. "But they've agreed to let me help. My job is to create a distraction with Sage while Tru and Embry come for you."

The threat hangs in the air between us—he'll be alone with Sage while Tru comes for me. Even if Sage is on her guard, she'll be in danger. He could do anything to her. The thought makes my skin go cold.

"You're going to help us," he states, holding the photo between us a moment more.

"What do you want me to do?" I ask, jaw almost too tight to speak.

"He wants Tru," Ryan says. I don't miss the way he pushes this off onto Anderson Flynn even though he's the one making sure it happens. "He needs her, understand?"

He places just enough emphasis on the word "needs" to tell me that Tru won't be hurt. At least not until Anderson Flynn gets what he wants.

"And we need you to make sure she chooses the southern stairwell for your escape," he continues, pointing south. "We'll do our best to make sure all other routes are cut off, but you're the fail-safe. If anything starts to go wrong, you make sure it doesn't."

"And how do I know you won't hurt my sister or anyone else?" I ask. "We haven't exactly established much trust."

"We don't need your trust," he says. "Just your cooperation."

I grind my teeth together to keep from saying anything I might regret. "And if I refuse?"

"Then you should know that Mr. Flynn doesn't do anything by halves."

The threat is both obscure and violently plain: Anderson Flynn won't just hurt Sage, he'll kill her.

Impotent fury gathers in the back of my throat like a storm. All my life, my actions have been determined by the whims and fears of others.

The song inside me begins to grow and I let it. I funnel its swift current into my hands, my wrists, where it grows hot. Maybe hot enough to melt steel or at least the plastic bedframe.

But then Ryan's hand is on mine, the melody of his song coursing through my mind, growing louder and stronger until it's all I can hear and my head aches with it.

This is not like it was at the river, when his song called to mine, running alongside with encouraging harmonies. This is dominating and discordant.

I try to pull away, but I'm held in place by the damned handcuffs and the force of his grip as my song drowns beneath his. I relent with a gasp.

"Can we agree that was a bad idea?" he asks, ducking low to peer directly into my face.

"I don't think we're ever going to agree on much," I snap.

"Right," he says. And then he steps forward so that he is too close, his face only a breath away from mine. "Then I will only tell you one more thing: Mr. Flynn is looking for his daughter."

My mind spins, reeling through this heady spike of anger toward more rational thought.

"I thought she was dead," I say, grasping.

"So did he," Ryan whispers. "But he has reason to believe that was a lie, that Logan Dire kidnapped her or worse. Now that the Ghoul has resurfaced."

"The Ghoul?" I ask, controlling my expression. "He died. Didn't you hear?"

"We heard," Ryan says, giving me a knowing smile. "But no one believes the Ghoul would be that easy to kill, do they?" He studies me for another second before adding, "Mr. Flynn wants to know what really happened to his daughter. He wants to know if she's alive and where she is."

"And he wants to kill the man responsible," I add. "Assuming he's still alive."

Ryan does me the courtesy of not denying it outright. "Wouldn't a kill like that be justified by Underhill law?"

"If it followed protocol," I say. "If it was true."

Ryan hesitates before adding, "Just know that this is about more than old grudges. And that I will do everything in my power to ensure no harm comes to Tru."

I pull back far enough that he can feel the full weight of my glare.

"It's your choice," he says. "You should be glad that he's giving it to you."

"Imagine my joy," I say through cold lips.

"You'll need this," he says, backing away to set something down on the shelf near the door, out of reach. A phone. *My* phone. "Good luck, whatever you choose."

And then he goes, leaving me alone with an impossible choice: Do I betray my girlfriend? Or my sister?

The Fifth Explosion of Lila Morgan

The day Ms. Jones told me I was ready to attend the gala was one of the best days of my life.

Her approval was like the light of the moon. Cool and ethereal and rarely felt. I craved it. Carefully, as with all things, because wanting something too much was a weakness.

I let Sage help me select a pantsuit that had shape without being too restrictive and a mask that looked like a flame—a promise that I would burn when I chose to. Testing was supposed to be anonymous, but that wasn't possible in my case. Even if there were other bombshells old enough to attend, I'm not sure they'd have been willing to go so soon after my father's accident.

Everyone knew that the bombshell in the room was Lila Morgan.

I heard whispers of "tick, tick, boom" when I stepped forward. The sound of it a quiet attack on my nerves.

I didn't mind. As Ms. Jones said, the louder they were, the easier it would be to prove them wrong.

When it was my turn, I entered the ring and Ms. Jones stepped down from her spot on the dais, joining me on the floor. That was the first thing to make me nervous.

"Number one-two-one," she called, though she could have just used my name. "You have listed your talent as 'bombshell,' a notoriously unstable talent. Your challenge will be to demonstrate how well you can control yourself under pressure."

I knew what was coming then, but there was nothing I could do about it. Ms. Jones attacked. Going all out with more skill than I'd ever experienced from her in our practice sessions. It was all I could do to react and defend.

Again and again, Ms. Jones attacked. She knocked me flat more than once, her fist a hammer I could not evade. Each time, I climbed to my feet and raised my fists.

I was nearly gasping for breath and bleeding in half a dozen places. I wanted nothing more than to drop to the floor and recover, but Ms. Jones was relentless.

At some point, I realized that the fight wasn't going to end until I did what I'd come there to do. I had to demonstrate my talent, not only my ability to hold it in check.

"Just like we've practiced," Ms. Jones whispered after knocking me to the ground once more.

With fatigue dragging at my focus, I climbed to my feet and stepped back from Ms. Jones. I knew exactly what she wanted from me.

The room seemed unnaturally quiet, as though everyone had suddenly left and Ms. Jones and I were alone. I knew it wasn't true, but I couldn't spare the energy to look. Instead, I closed my eyes and concentrated on the control I had left. I felt the note of my talent hum along my skin, and I focused on letting just enough of it out that it wouldn't run away with me.

Then I did exactly what Ms. Jones had taught me to do. With every muscle in my body alight with tension, I released my control for just a second, letting my talent pulse from my core.

I felt the force of it, saw Ms. Jones fly back, her body knocking against the security field before hitting the floor. And that was it.

When I opened my eyes again, I was lying on a cot in Underhill's clinic, and the world had changed.

Ms. Jones leaned over me, pride glowing in her expression. "Welcome to the Underhill Apprentice Program, Lila Morgan," she said. "We're going to do great things together."

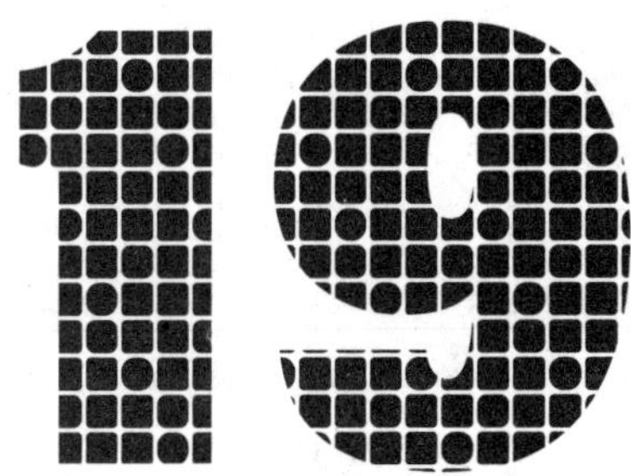

When Sage and I were little, we used to play a game we creatively called escape. It was both very simple and very elaborate.

The task was always the same: get from point A to B without being spotted. But what counted as being spotted changed depending on where we were, who we were with, even the time of day and the weather. If it was after dark and we were outside, being tagged by the headlight of a car counted; during the day, eye contact was king.

Being handcuffed to this bed is kind of the opposite. The guard's eyes only ever leave me for a split second when he gets a message on his phone or there's a coded knock at the door.

Ryan thinks that my only option for fighting back is too dangerous to consider. But I can't sit here and wait for my friends to rescue me. Especially not if it means Tru will take my place.

I'm never out of the cuffs either: both wrists chained to the bed when it's just me and the guard, hands cuffed together when the nurse is here and I need more mobility. The only time I know I'll be out of everyone's line of sight is when I'm actually peeing or in the shower. Even then, the nurse doesn't close the door all the way, tracking my movements with her ears. But I can work with that.

The second the bathroom door swings partly closed, I do exactly what I tried and failed to do earlier. The song surges into my mind and heat follows. It's so sudden that I break into a sweat and have to squeeze my eyes tight to maintain focus. I funnel the song, easing the volume back and driving it into my hands and wrists, willing it to be hot enough to—

The snap of steel breaks my concentration. For a second all I can do is stare down at the chain that once linked my handcuffs together and now hangs divided.

"What was that?" the nurse asks, the door already swinging toward me.

I have only an instant to think before I move. I shove the door back at her as hard as I can. There's a satisfying crack as it connects with her face and a muffled gasp to go with it.

I know the guard inside the room is probably on his feet already, so I yank the door open. The surprise on the nurse's face is quickly vanishing, but I have just enough time to press my advantage.

She's on the ground in two moves, but those two moves take a second too long and I'm hit from behind.

Stars explode in my vision. I duck, anticipating the attack that will come next. Swivel and sweep. My leg connects with something, but not well enough. I blink, willing my vision to clear.

I see shadows and light, the shape of the guard catching his balance and turning toward me once more.

I'm still in the bathroom, with limited room to fight, much less run. I'm practically in the shower—the very definition of being backed into a corner. And then I realize that it's a corner with a shower curtain. One designed to tear away easily.

In one movement, I pull it free and yank it over my attacker's head and shoulders.

He moves suddenly, with all the speed of a wingtip, but I don't let go and he goes down, hitting the ground on his knees. I draw back, preparing to deliver a blow, but someone beats me to it.

A shadow looms in the door. There's a grunt, and my attacker slumps against the plastic curtain and doesn't move again.

And when I look up, I find a somewhat familiar but instantly recognizable face looking back at me.

"Hello, Lila Morgan," Logan Dire says, and holds a length

of rubber tubing out to me. The kind used for IV bags. "They won't be out for long. Help me bind them, please."

I do exactly as he says because while I have a lot of questions right now, none of them are about this man's priorities.

We make quick work of tying up the nurse and the guard who attacked me. Before we lock them in the bathroom, Logan hauls in another unconscious guard.

"There was one outside," he explains as he binds the man's hands and adds him to our bathroom collection.

I'm strangely relieved to see that it's not Ryan. Also, not so strangely disappointed.

Hospital bathroom doors aren't exactly designed to lock from the outside, but Logan is miles ahead of that problem. He pulls a fork out of his pocket—which I assume he pilfered from somewhere in the hallway—and expertly snaps the head off so it's in two pieces.

I've heard about this method before, but I've never seen it in action. Logan doesn't even pause as he bends the tines, jams them into the latch, and pulls the door shut before securing it all in place by driving the detached handle back through the tines.

"That won't hold them much longer than the binds," he says, eyes scanning the room for anything else that might be useful.

Every move he makes is intentional and sure, entirely different from the guy I only ever knew as "Sage's best friend's dad." It's easy to see how this version of Logan inspired so much fear and almost reverence over the years.

He is all competence and strength.

He's also covered in cuts and bruises, and he's not quite managing to hide that he's favoring his left leg.

"What happened to you?" I ask.

He meets my eyes and shakes his head. "There's no time for explanations. We need to get you out of here."

I point to the door. "You just created a padlock out of a fork. I agree we're in a hurry, but we can talk while we run."

He ignores this and moves to the door of the room. He eases it open just far enough that he can spy on the hallway outside and watches for twenty seconds before easing it shut once more.

"Talking will slow down our running. If Tru arrives before you leave here, we will be in a much less favorable situation," he says, voice calm even though he's arguing with me. "I presume you agree with that or you wouldn't have been attempting to escape on your own."

"How do you know Tru is coming?" I ask.

His lips tighten. It's not much of a reaction, but coming from Logan, I'm inclined to think it represents vast internal turmoil.

"Because," he says in a tone that's more car engine than voice. "I've been their prisoner for the past week."

"A week?" I can't hide my surprise. "I thought they needed Tru to flush you out of hiding."

He shakes his head, grim-faced. "They need Tru to get me to talk."

"I guess that's lucky for me," I say. "Thank you for your help."

Logan nods and checks the hallway again. "They will know I'm gone by now and someone will come to check on you soon. We are on the fifth floor and there is a lot of additional security on this level. We need to take the stairs straight down to the main floor and from there to the parking garage."

He lists it all out like these are the steps in a recipe. All we have to do is complete them in order and at the end we'll have cake.

Except it's never that simple.

"Your boots are over there." He points without looking.

"Don't all exits on high-security wards come with alarms?" I ask as I retrieve my boots and quickly put them on. "Five flights of stairs is a lot of distance to cover, especially if we're alerting the troops at the very beginning. And I'm not a wingtip."

Logan turns to me, keeping the door propped. "I'm going to have to ask you to hold on tightly."

It takes me a second to grasp his meaning. When I do, my stomach flips.

"You want me to hold on to . . . you?"

"I do," he confirms. "I will do my best to ensure you reach the parking garage safely. Once we're there, I will distract them while you escape."

My jaw drops at this. But only briefly. "No. Absolutely not. We're going together."

"We cannot," he answers.

"We can. And we will. Because Tru deserves to see her father again and she might not forgive me if I have to tell her that I left without him."

"I'm afraid it has to be this way," he answers.

"Why?" I demand, struggling to keep my voice down, but I'm angry now.

"Because." His lips tighten again, revealing something that might be regret. "If I leave with you now, we'll be right back where we started and they will be more confident than ever that the way to me—and what I know—is through her."

"But she would have *you*, and—"

"And she does not deserve to bear the burdens of my past," Logan interjects, his voice louder than it's been. "I need to finish this. And I will. But I cannot do it with her in danger."

The argument fizzles in my throat. I can't blame him for protecting his daughter. And I sure as hell can't stop him.

"Are you ready?" he asks, checking the hall once more.

I nod and then remember my phone, left by Ryan where I wouldn't be able to reach it until I'd escaped. I shove it into my pocket and return to Logan, taking his outstretched hand. "We need to avoid the south stairwell," I say. "That's where they wanted me to guide Tru."

Logan nods and just before he opens the door, I ask, "Is Anderson's daughter still alive?"

Logan's fingers tighten around mine, but his expression goes solid as a mountain face. At first I think he won't answer me, and then he says, "I don't know."

With that, he pulls the door open and we step out into the hall.

I knew that I was being held inside a hospital, but it's still startling to find myself in one. The hallway outside my room is broad and shiny and lined with doors that all look the same. The air smells hollow and clean, and I can hear muffled voices from behind mostly closed doors. The whole place is going about its daily existence while I'm about to make a jailbreak with Kansas City's most storied Enforcer.

Before I've fully registered what's happening, Logan has draped my arm across his shoulders and pulled me onto his back. He manages it with such ease that I hardly notice my feet have left the ground before we're moving. Flying. So fast that the hall blurs in my vision.

I know that my arms are wrapped around his neck and

I'm sure it isn't comfortable for him, but I don't dare adjust my grip or move in any way. Every muscle in my body is clenched tight as I do my best to be more like a jacket on his back than a parachute slowing him down.

I feel an impact as we collide with the emergency stairs, but we've already descended a full flight before I hear the alarm sound. It blasts through the stairwell like a tornado siren, and maybe it's because we're moving so fast, but it seems much louder than it should.

Logan grunts as he throws one shoulder into the next door, and then we're running through the lobby too fast for anyone to confirm what it was that just brushed their back.

In seconds more we're in the parking garage, where the air is noticeably more humid and smells like wet asphalt instead of that very specific bleach hospitals use on every single surface.

Logan still doesn't stop. His pace increases. The world blurs. My stomach churns. And I wonder how all the wingtips I've ever known got used to this nauseating view of the world.

Maybe some of them take Dramamine. I think I would have to.

I suddenly realize Logan is checking over his shoulder. Not looking for danger but tracking it.

We're being followed.

I turn my head to look and instantly know it was a mistake. Nausea sweeps over me and I have to grit my teeth against a sudden and embarrassing desire to vomit.

I can't think of anything worse than vomiting on my

girlfriend's dad. Except maybe vomiting on the Ghoul of Kansas City.

Logan cuts left so abruptly I nearly lose my grip. The air changes again, and I feel the heat of the sun against my skin as we pass out of the garage. And then he stops.

My feet hit the ground, but the world still feels like it's moving. Logan keeps one hand on my arm, seeming to understand that not everyone is used to moving at super speeds.

"Deep breaths," he says. "It will pass."

I can hear what he's not saying. It needs to pass. Quickly. He's put distance between us and our pursuer, but they're still out there.

"I'm good," I say, but I don't let go of his arm. "We can go."

"You can go," he clarifies. "I'll lead them away."

A protest is on the tip of my tongue, but I can see the determination in his eyes, and I doubt anything has changed in the five minutes since the last time we had this argument.

"Okay," I say.

"Good. Do you recognize your surroundings?" he asks.

I almost smile. Tru has mentioned that Logan has a habit of sounding like he belongs in a fantasy novel, and now I understand what she meant.

We've stopped strategically, between two houses set close together. They're typical KC bungalow-style houses in varying states of repair. Between that, the lack of driveways, and the fact that I was just in a hospital, I make an educated guess.

"Hospital Hill," I say.

He nods once, eyes surveying the street in either direction.

"I trust you can make your way from here. You need to get to Tru and the others before they leave to rescue you, and then you need to take them all to Underhill. Can you do that?"

I nod at the same moment a sleek black car turns onto the street and pauses. Headlights aimed at us like the eyes of a predator.

Logan finally lets me go.

"I believe we've run out of time," he says.

A sudden press of tears clogs my throat. I have known Logan through rumor and reputation and then through Tru, never from my own experience. Until now. And after barely fifteen minutes in his presence, I already know that he is as good as Tru believes him to be. He is worth fighting for.

And right now, I can't do that.

"Run, Lila," he says, turning to look at me with soft blue eyes. "Run and tell Tru that I love her."

"Would you change your mind if I say I wouldn't?" I ask, fighting to keep my voice from trembling.

His face softens into a sorrowful smile. "It has been a pleasure knowing you, Lila Morgan."

He runs toward the car. He isn't moving at full speed and the limp in his left leg is noticeable.

I stare for a second too long, long enough to see three men pour out of the car and grab Logan. He fights, but I can tell it's mostly for show.

My eyes stick on the license plate as a voice in my head screams that if I get myself caught, too, this will have been for nothing.

My task now is to intercept Tru before she can put herself in danger and get her to Underhill.

I run, darting between houses and over chain-link fences, checking street names until I reach one I know and can map a course to Tru's house. I focus on the mundane task of planning my route and not on what is happening to Logan, but my heart aches with every step.

And then I remember that my phone is in my pocket. I don't have to race home; I just have to reach Tru before she leaves it.

The phone is fully charged, which almost tricks me into having a good feeling about Ryan until I remember that he didn't do it for me. He did it *to* me.

I unlock the phone and call Tru.

It rings once, twice. "Lila!"

I hear a commotion in the background and Sage's voice repeating my name. Asking if I'm okay. Demanding to know where I am.

"I'm putting you on speaker," Tru says. "Lila? Lila, are you still there?"

I open my mouth to say that I am, but no sound comes out.

"Lila?" Sage's voice. "Lila! Say something!"

I try again, swallowing past the threat of completely unwarranted tears. "Still here," I manage. "I'm okay."

There's a garble of sound and static as Tru and Sage attempt to speak at the same time and then Tru's voice comes through again.

"There's something we need to tell you," she says.

"Wait, the guy you've been talking to, the one with blond hair and tattoos?" I ask, urgency spurring me on. "Don't trust him. Don't do anything he suggested. We have to get to Underhill, okay? Can you meet me there?"

"Lila," Tru says, voice softer now. "You can't go to Underhill."

"What do you mean?" I ask.

I hear her words, but they go soft around the edges. All sound and no form. I feel numb and strange, like the world changed while I was inside my little hospital room prison cell and this is just a dream.

"Did you hear her?" Sage is asking. "Lila! Are you still there, Lila?"

"I'm here," I say though partially numb lips. "What did you say?"

"You can't go to Underhill," Tru says again, her voice firm enough to ground me this time. "Because they've put a bounty on you."

I hear the words this time, but it does nothing to dislodge the numb stillness that has fallen over me. I'm not shaking anymore. I'm not crying or even on the edge of crying. I'm just quiet. Stunned.

But not confused.

There's a bounty.

On me.

With perfect calm, I pull up BountyApp. The active bounties tab is alight with notifications. But the most recent is all about me.

> **FIND BOUNTY:** *SPARROW*
>
> *To be returned to Underhill for the evasion of Underhill bombshell polices.*

REWARD: *$50,000*

SPONSOR: *Underhill, Inc.*

I read it once and then I close the app.

The pulse monitor is still sitting on the table in my hospital room. I think again that if we hadn't hacked it before our date, it might have been the thing that led to an earlier rescue.

If anyone cared.

That, I realize, is what Ryan was trying to tell me. I am working to gain the respect of people and an organization that will never care enough to respect me back.

When they realized the monitor wasn't working, they didn't spend an ounce of time wondering if something had happened to me.

They made me an outlaw.

"Lila?" Tru asks.

"*You* need to get to Underhill," I repeat.

There is so much I need to tell her, so much she deserves to know, but I feel hollow and drained and like I'm running out of options.

"Don't worry about us. We're fine. Ryan isn't here," she says. I can hear panic edging into her voice. "Can you get to us? Where are you?"

The urge to go home to be with all of them is overwhelming. I want nothing more than to be in the kitchen with Tru and Sage and Embry and Amethyst while everyone makes dinner despite Sage's attempts to oversalt things. I want to hide my smiles when Amethyst teases Embry or Sage pretends to get angry about something completely ridiculous. I want to hold Tru's hand and plan another date.

But I promised Logan that I would get Tru to Underhill, get her to safety while he took care of things. Going home would put her—and Sage and Amethyst and Embry—in danger.

"I don't think I can," I say.

I realize that I'm still headed toward Tru's house and turn left. I have to keep moving, even though there's nowhere for me to go. There's a bounty on my head. Sooner or later, someone will find me.

"Are you hurt?" Sage nearly shouts. "Don't lie to me, Lila Morgan, or I will go up to our room right now and cut a hole in every single shirt you own."

That makes me smile. "I'm not hurt," I say. "But I won't put you in danger. You all need to get to Underhill. Fast. I'll explain it later, but please just trust me and do it."

"Why?" Tru asks with a note of suspicion now. "What aren't you telling us?"

"There's no time to explain." I feel a pang at the echo of my conversation with Logan an hour ago.

"I think we should make time," Tru says stubbornly. "Make us understand."

I close my eyes in frustration for a second. I know what will happen if I tell her the truth and it doesn't involve getting her safely to Underhill. But if I don't tell her the truth, there's a decent chance I still won't get her safely to Underhill.

I take a deep breath. "They have Logan."

The silence on the other end of the line is thick. I picture all four of them clustered around the phone held out in Tru's hand, their expressions ranging from wild surprise on Sage's face to calm acknowledgment on Amethyst's. It's Tru's face I can't picture.

"He got me out," I continue. "But they still have him. It's why they wanted you, Tru, and not me. And I doubt that's changed, so you need to get where they can't reach you. Is Embry there?"

"I'm here." His voice comes through loud and clear.

"Amethyst?" I ask.

"Listening to every word," he confirms.

"Tru and Sage are going to try and convince you to come look for me, and I need you to promise me you won't let them," I say. "Okay?"

"Are you going to cover our hospital bills?" Embry asks, but I can hear by the tone of his voice that he's accepted the mission.

"We've got this, Lie," Amethyst says.

"Wait, did you just give her a nickname?" Sage interjects, incensed. "That's a best friend thing. Did you two become best friends without telling me?"

"Not really the time for this, Sage," Embry says.

"Lila is currently trying to convince us to abandon her so she can go into deep cover or something," Sage argues. "I'm pretty sure now is the time for literally everything."

"Is he okay?" Tru's voice again, snarled with worry.

"He's okay," I say. "But I don't think he will be for long."

"What do they want from him?"

"Answers," I say, wishing I could lie instead. "About Anderson's daughter. They think she's alive."

Another silence follows and this one tells me that they haven't spent the past three days just waiting around for me to get back. They've been gathering intel.

"What is it?" I ask.

"She was supposedly buried here in Kansas City," Sage reports. "But we've searched everywhere and there's no grave."

"No grave," I repeat. "Do you think that means—"

"There's no body? Because, yeah, that has definitely crossed our minds," Sage says. "The problem is we can't prove any of it and until now, we didn't know why it mattered."

"But if she's alive and Logan knows where she is, it matters a lot," Tru adds.

I don't bother saying that it doesn't matter if Logan knows or not. It only matters if Anderson Flynn *thinks* Logan knows. Or can find out.

I also don't bother saying that Logan is only useful to him while Flynn believes that to be true.

I try to think past that: Why wasn't Flynn's daughter dead as everyone had been led to believe?

And why wouldn't Logan want to clear his name by reuniting her with her family?

"You think he's protecting her," I say. "You think he's protecting her *from Flynn.* They were going to use you to force him to reveal her, but she doesn't want to be found."

"That's exactly what I think," Tru answers.

"Then you *really* have to get to Underhill. They'll protect you and I'll—"

"What? Stay out in the cold? Go into hiding like Anderson Flynn's daughter? This is ridiculous," Tru says. "Lila, tell us where you are or tell us where to meet you. We'll come to you and we'll go to Underhill together and we will make them understand."

"Because you trust them now?" I ask bitterly.

"Because we trust you," she corrects.

I grip the phone a little too tightly and it slips from my grasp, hitting the ground hard enough to split the screen. Scooping it up, I spot a sleek gray car moving down the street in my direction. I move on instinct, slipping behind a thick tree trunk as it passes. Nothing about it sets off any alarms in my mind, but it does remind me of something.

Tru and Sage are calling my name when I press the phone to my ear again.

"I'm here," I say. "And I'm fine. I need you to believe that I'm fine and that it's better if I don't come to you yet, okay?"

Silence follows so I continue.

"We can't help Logan if we're all focused on hiding me. You have to trust that I'm okay and get to Underhill and put a find bounty on the car that took him. We track him that way and maybe we can get to him in time to help him."

"You got the plate?" Tru breathes.

"Of course I got the plate," I say. "Do you trust that I'm okay?"

After another brief silence, she responds, "I trust you."

"Okay," I say, unprepared for how those three words land in my chest. "Then, I think we have a plan."

The Sixth Explosion of Lila Morgan

Ms. Jones and I did do great things together. For several years, my talent was more a threat than a reality, one I kept under rigid control. It wasn't until Tru that the cracks started to show. The great things Ms. Jones wanted to do were rooted in resentment and anger. In a belief that bombshells, with the assistance of bastion blood, deserved to rule over all the others.

It was a darkness I didn't see until it was almost too late.

Until Tru and I were locked in cells in the basement of a seemingly abandoned warehouse in the West Bottoms and Ms. Jones was on her way to install herself as the supreme leader of Underhill.

We realized at the same moment that if we wanted to stop her and save Boss Acosta, we were going to have to take desperate measures. Namely, that I was going to have to go full bombshell and hope Tru's talent for surviving meant she could endure it and still be capable of going after Ms. Jones.

"I can't take that risk," I said, already having a hard enough time controlling my emotions.

All I could think about was all those years ago in the field with my father. The surge of anger I'd felt then wasn't so different from the maelstrom inside me now, and my failure to control my talent had led to the death of that small deer.

"Lila," Tru answered. I saw her hand reach out through the bars of her cell, searching for mine.

I braided my fingers through hers. The warmth of her touch was grounding. "I don't want to hurt you," I admitted.

"You can't," she said. Matter of fact.

I was glad she couldn't see my face in that moment. There was no amount of control that could stop my anguish from showing there. Maybe it was Tru. As a bastion, Tru had survived dozens of things that would kill someone without her talent, but I was certain that standing next to an imploding star was different.

Even so, it was the only way.

Having exhausted our options, Tru got as far from the wall separating our cells as possible and I stood in the center of mine. I took deep breaths and did my best to still the fear in my heart.

It's strange, but in that moment, I couldn't help but think of my father and the first night my talent had presented. And for some reason, the detail that came into hyperfocus for the first time was the fact that there had been no damage to the living room. Not to the walls or furniture, not even to the carpet beneath my feet.

There had only been me and my father with his arms around me. The strange pulse between us. And the promise that maybe there was more to being a bombshell than anyone knew.

The thought calmed me, clarified my mind enough that with another deep breath, I released the vise grip I maintained over my talent and let it grow.

My part of the plan is the worst because all I have to do is not get found. That means lying low until there's something to be done. But lying low is always so much harder than it sounds. Especially when you're low on resources.

A few months ago, I had an apartment that no one knew existed, stocked with everything I might need. It gave me an amazing vantage point over the city, and it had five ways in and out.

If I still had it, I could have a shower, a change of clothes, and a meal that didn't taste like low-calorie rubber.

Instead, I have to find somewhere to hide where the many bounty hunters on my trail won't think to look for me.

I've worked hard to be both exceedingly predictable and utterly unknowable. People associate me with Underhill, Ms. Jones, my sister, and now with Tru. That means there are very specific places they might expect me to be in moments of crisis. But people also associate me with having an excessively level head, so they might expect me to avoid those places.

With a bounty on me, the least obvious place for me to seek any kind of shelter is on Underhill's doorstep. No one would expect me to put myself anywhere near the very organization that is looking for me. Because it would be utterly foolish.

I wasn't lying when I told the others I couldn't come with them *to* Underhill, and yet it's exactly where I go. Backtracking frequently enough to ensure I'm not being followed, I make my meandering way to Union Station.

The summer sun is well past its zenith, and without any hint of cloud cover, the city is hot. I detour through the Crown Center mall, dodging tourists and teens out of school for the summer, and duck into the bathroom. My clothing was three days stale before I started walking, and I'm pretty sure I smell like an overripe gym bag by now. There's not much I can do about it, but I can take a minute to address my appearance.

My nurse was kind enough to allow me a shower at the midway point in my captivity, so at least my hair isn't a complete grease bomb. I look overdressed for the middle of the day in clothes I wore for my date with Tru: blue blouse, black miniskirt, and ankle boots with a heel. I also look like I've been sleeping in these clothes for several days. Which I have.

The best I can do is smooth my hair into a proper bun, splash a little water on my face, and tuck in my blouse more purposefully. The end result is passable and not so out of place that I'll attract too much attention.

As I leave the restroom, I hit a wall of scent—sweet and smoky barbeque, salty French fries, chocolate notes drifting on top of it all—and my stomach growls. I walk faster, desperate to get away from the distraction of hunger.

A small voice reminds me that hunger like this will chip away at my control and make me a danger to everyone around me. But a louder one insists that I'm bigger than my fears and can eat after I survive this.

Union Station appears as I round the corner, its arms spread wide like wings. It has always struck me as a welcoming place. Underhill accepted me when it felt like no one else would, and Ms. Jones made it feel like it could be a home when I had none. They told me that as long as I followed the rules, it would always be there for me.

I fooled myself into believing that Underhill's rules meant something. That they could keep me safe even when I couldn't do that for myself.

But that was always a lie.

Underhill's rules have only ever been to keep Underhill safe. As soon as it perceived me as a threat, the rules changed.

I stop across the street from the station and step back from the curb. The crosswalk light turns green, then red. Green, then red, and still I stand there.

It takes me a few seconds to realize that my phone is ringing. I answer without looking.

"Did they find it already?" I ask eagerly, a little surprised at how quickly they tracked the car.

"Find what?"

Ryan. His voice has etched itself into my mind.

He sighs when I don't respond. In the background I can hear the sounds of traffic. I scan the space around me, searching for any sign of his blond hair. My eyes snag on someone tall enough to be him with a phone pressed to his ear, but he raises a cigarette and takes a long drag. Ryan has never carried the stink of smoke.

"Don't worry, wherever you are, I haven't found you yet," he says. "I'd be a little disappointed if I had. It was an impressive escape you pulled off. Mr. Flynn agrees."

The admiration in his voice is real. I can almost hear him smiling.

"I had help," I say, starting to move again. This time I go away from Union Station. Stepping inside its echoing chambers would tell Ryan much more about where I am than sounds of traffic possibly could.

"You did," he agrees. "And it's lucky for all of us that he decided to stay rather than run. This would all have gotten a little . . . messier if he'd gone with you. Of course, now we're kind of back where we started."

"Leave Tru alone," I say through clenched teeth.

"I didn't call you to talk about Tru," he says. "I called to talk about this bounty on your head. I assume you know about it or you'd have already made a statement to Underhill."

"And?"

"And I'm sorry things turned out this way, though I'm not surprised. I don't think you are, either." He pauses, giving me space to agree with him. I don't answer. "Mr. Flynn's offer is still on the table. In fact, he's even more interested in hiring you now that you've demonstrated your resourcefulness. I gather that you took down two of our agents. And since we only hire the best, that makes you even more appealing."

"I'm not a piece of meat," I spit.

Ryan laughs. "No, Lila, I think you are the sharp edge of a knife."

"I've already told you I'm not joining you," I say.

"You did, but that was before the bounty," he answers quickly. "Things have changed and so has the deal. As a signing bonus, Mr. Flynn will make sure that bounty disappears."

I stop in my tracks. "How?"

"Proprietary methods," he says.

That means Mr. Flynn can cut a deal with Underhill. That Underhill would willingly, reliably cut a deal with Mr. Flynn. That Underhill would break their own rules for the right price.

Or the right blackmail.

My head spins with the injustice of it all. The fickle impermanence of it all.

If Underhill is this mutable, maybe it would be better to work for someone like Mr. Flynn, where the rules may be biased but at least they aren't pretending to be something they aren't.

Maybe then, my very presence wouldn't constantly put the people I love and care about in danger.

"He'll take care of the bounty, and as soon as he has what he needs from Mr. Dire, we'll get you set up in Las Vegas. It's not the greatest weather, but there's plenty of space for us to exercise our talents."

"What he needs from Mr. Dire," I repeat, more to myself than to him, but he answers anyway.

"It would have been easier with your help, but Mr. Flynn always gets what he wants."

"Like the location of his daughter," I say.

"Yes, exactly."

This situation has felt off from the beginning. From the moment Anna Mirth told us that Logan killed Mr. Flynn's daughter, the pieces just haven't fit together. I believe Tru when she says Logan wouldn't have killed a child, but if he didn't, how could someone with as many resources as Mr. Flynn be so convinced he did? Why would Logan never clear his name?

"If Mr. Flynn's daughter is alive, why hasn't she come to find him?" I ask.

"Because her supposed killer botched the job and if she were revealed to be alive, he'd come fix his mistake," Ryan answers quickly.

"With how powerful you keep telling me Mr. Flynn is, he wouldn't be able to protect her from one man? Never mind," I add quickly. "What if you have that backward?" I ask. "What if she's been hiding because she's afraid of her father?"

"Why on earth would she be afraid of him?" he fires back.

"That's a good question," I say. "I think we should find out."

"How do you think you're going to do that?" he asks.

For a split second I have no idea, and then the answer is there.

I know who Anderson's daughter is, and I know how to find her.

"Proprietary methods," I say.

"Li—" he starts, but I hang up.

I turn back toward Union Station and Underhill with a plan.

The real beauty of discovering someone's most cherished secret is how effortlessly it opens doors.

It's why people like Anderson Flynn have so much power in the world. Everyone has something they'd rather not come to light. Even an organization like Underhill.

Tru doesn't ask questions when I text to ask for Anna Mirth's number. She sends it with an update:

Headed to UH now. Stay sharp.

I breathe a little easier and dial the number.

Anna answers on the first ring. "Who is this?"

I'd considered using a voice-distorting app, but decided

there really wasn't any point. I wasn't doing this to stay anonymous.

"This is Lila Morgan," I say. "We met a few days ago."

"I remember," she says, a hint of wariness in her voice. "I heard you'd gone missing."

"That happens when you're grabbed by Anderson Flynn's people," I agree. "They meant to grab Tru and I'm sure you can guess why."

There's a beat of silence before she asks, "Do they have him?"

"They have him," I say, preparing to leverage what I think I know. "I'm sure he won't tell anyone about you."

She gasps.

I've guessed correctly, so I continue. "But I might."

I let the implication hang between us. My words are a statement, a request, and a threat all in one, even if I have no intention of telling anyone who she really is.

"Lila," she starts, but I cut her off.

"We need to talk," I say. "In person. Meet me in the main gallery of Union Station in ten minutes. Or I take what I know straight to Underhill."

"There's a bounty on your head," she points out, hoping to call my bluff.

But I was prepared for this.

"Logan's life is more important than a bounty," I say. And then I hang up.

As I step through the doors, the sun dips low in the sky, washing Union Station's vast entryway in molten copper light. There are a few security guards lingering around the stairwell and information booth, the open-air restaurant in the middle is filling with diners, and tourists shuffle this way and that with their cameras raised. It's enough to ensure that two people strolling through the main gallery won't be out of place.

Anna arrives in eight minutes flat and joins me in the wide space, broadcasting her nervousness by the way she twists her hands before her. The surface differences are obvious—Anna's skin is brown and her salt-and-pepper hair is braided into thick ropes that twist into a bun, and I doubt Anderson Flynn has ever thought to wring his hands—now that I know to look for it, I see the resemblance right away. They have the same long nose and wide mouth, the same arch to the eyebrows.

She presses her lips together as she approaches me, concern deepening in the bend of her brow. "I know what you want me to do, and I'm very sorry but I can't."

I expected this. If she were prepared to come forward, I think she would have done it a long time ago.

"I know you're afraid," I start, but she's already shaking her head.

"You don't understand," she says, voice quiet and tense. "I have been hiding since the day Logan saved my life. He made sure that I would never be in danger again. I've lived a good life, but when I saw what Tru was brave enough to do, I thought maybe I could do that, too."

"What does Tru have to do with this?" I ask.

Anna catches her breath, eyes widening as she realizes that I hadn't deciphered the whole puzzle and we're standing on the precipice of yet another secret.

And then I do work it out. "You're a bastion, too."

She nods. It changes everything so quickly that I can hardly keep up with my own thoughts.

"The bounty all those years ago was a setup," I say as the last pieces come together. "Your father was *trying* to get you killed."

"That's what Logan always thought, but could never prove," Anna says, nodding. "It wasn't Logan who took my father's bounty originally—it was Tru's mother. She was able to save my life when everything went sideways, but at that point we were both marked. And my father doesn't like to lose."

"So she went to Logan," I say, filling in the gaps. "And he faked your death? Put you in hiding?"

There's a flurry of noise from the opposite end of the gallery. Both Anna and I turn, our nerves alight, but it's just a group of teens messing around.

"Wait. Why was your father trying to kill you?" I ask.

"Because of what I am," she answers sadly. "My mother kept it hidden, dosing me with lavender to ensure I wouldn't accidentally reveal myself. But the problem with living a lie when you're that young is that eventually you're going to test the boundaries. I skipped a dose, just to see what would happen."

I almost want to tell her to stop. She doesn't have to confess all this to me.

Except I need to know.

"My father, as it turns out, not only fears bastions, but saw me as an Achilles' heel," she says. "He was convinced that if anyone found out his daughter was a bastion, he'd lose everything. He would be untrustworthy by association, every member of his family forever suspect."

She goes silent and after a minute, I bring the conversation back to the present.

"And you thought, with everything that was changing, you might be able to come out of hiding? That Underhill might protect you?"

She nods, tears returning to her eyes. "But I was wrong. I reached out to my mother, thinking she would help me, but I was wrong. I didn't realize how frightened she was and still is of him. She couldn't even bear the thought of keeping my secret. My mother revealed me to my father, exposed what Logan had done, and then—" She stops to collect herself.

For a moment I'm struck by the enormity of that betrayal. My own mother left me and Sage on our own, but even that doesn't compare to the brutal reality of being turned over like this. What must it have been like to grow up knowing you could never trust your own parents?

What might have happened to Tru if her parents had looked at her with this much fear?

"I came back to Kansas City to find Logan. To warn him," Anna says, swallowing her tears back. "To tell him that I messed up. As long as I stayed hidden, I was safe. But I broke that peace when I told my mother what had happened, and now my father will kill anyone who knows the truth. Even talking to you puts you in danger."

"That's exactly why you should help us," I say. "If you tell Underhill who you are and what has happened, your father won't be able to do anything about it. Everything will come out."

"And nothing will happen to him," she answers with conviction. "I'm alive, which means Logan didn't actually commit any crime. Even if he had, my father has made a career of getting away with things. Underhill doesn't want a war between talents. They won't be able to touch him and then one day, when no one is looking, I'll just vanish. For real this time."

Fear shows in the tremble of her hands. For a second, I'm struck by the tragic absurdity of it; that someone whose talent prevents them from being injured is this afraid of a single person. It's almost as absurd as fearing an entire group of people based on the actions of one.

Almost as absurd as hiding the beauty of a talent because someone, somewhere might see it as a threat.

It's all driven by fear, and that's not how I want to live.

"He might do those things," I say. "It's possible, and we can't know for sure until it happens. But we do know that he has Logan, and that he will kill him if they can't find you. And he will still come after you, because you are a loose end."

My phone buzzes in my pocket, the chime of a text muffled against the fabric of my skirt. I tug it free and glance down to see a message from Tru:

> *Our find bounty was claimed! The car is parked at the World War I memorial. Meet us there.*

My stomach dips, at once anxious and eager. The memorial is right across the street. Logan is so close. Even if I can't convince Anna to speak up, maybe I can still save his life.

"I know what it's like to be afraid of the world. And I know what it's like to believe that you're alone. It's hard to stand up when there is so much power telling you where to sit. But the thing about power is that it isn't fixed. We have our own even if it doesn't feel like it. And we can use it, but we have to choose." I press on. "Your father wants you to believe you shouldn't get to live, but why would you ever do what he wants again?"

I meet Anna's eyes. Still frightened and so used to hiding.

"The car they took him in is at the memorial across the street," I say, gesturing toward the front doors. "I think he's there, too, and I'm going to fight for him. Because not only does your dad not deserve to win, but Logan doesn't deserve to lose."

Without waiting for an answer, I turn and I go.

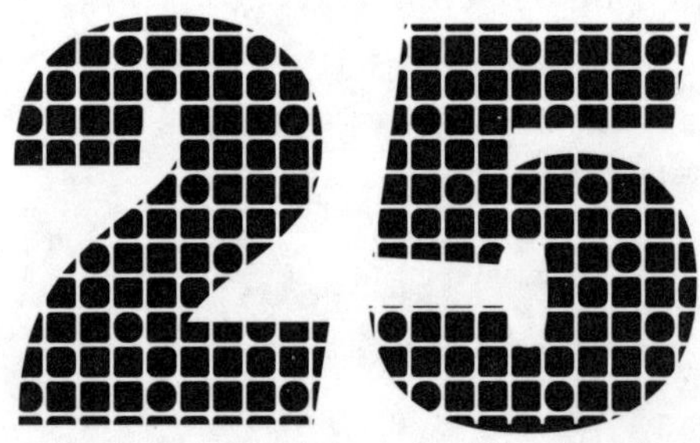

The sun is beginning to set and city lights shine orange and blue and pale gold along the streets. I run straight up the hill toward the towering World War I memorial. It stretches up against a black sky, pale sandstone lit from above and below. At the very top, an ocher flame flickers in the twilight, occasionally disappearing from view as something moves in front of it.

As I get closer, I recognize the shape of a person standing on the railing. His arms appear to be bound in front of him and his feet are braced wide for balance. He shifts this way and that as the breeze picks up strength. One wrong move and he would tip over the edge, plunging however many feet onto the stone below.

Logan.

I can't see his face, but I know it's him. And I know he's not alone up there. Someone is forcing him to stand there, on the very brink of a fatal fall.

I crest the hill in time to see Embry's car racing down the long drive toward the memorial. He swings around the bend, coming to a bruising stop behind the only other car on the drive, the same one that took Logan earlier today.

The doors of Embry's car open and Tru races to the other car, peering through the windows even though there's no real chance Logan is still inside. She has to check.

All of a sudden, it occurs to me to wonder why the car is still there. They've had time to get Logan from the vehicle to the top of the tower. Why leave anything behind that might point to your location—unless you're laying a trap.

I watch Amethyst clock Logan's position at the top of the tower and shout for Tru to look. I watch Sage raise her phone to record this moment. I watch Embry scan the grounds and spot me, his eyes going wide and relieved.

And I watch five dark-clad figures close in around them.

I scream, but too late to do anything other than distract Tru. Her eyes find me when they should be finding the figures approaching from behind.

I run toward her and Sage and Embry and Amethyst, but I'm too late.

Flynn's men are prepared for this. They designed it, staged it so they could grab Tru, which I made possible—inevitable—when I gave her the car's plates.

I betrayed her after all.

The figures close in, indistinguishable due to facial scrubbers except for one—Ryan. He surges forward, rushing into the melee, and lobs something at Tru. It looks like a glass grenade and when it bursts at her feet, it releases a cloud of smoke. Even at this distance, the smell of lavender is overwhelming.

I lose Tru in the smoke. The next time I see her, she's locked in a struggle with Ryan, matching every move with one of her own. And then I see something else: a mask fitted tightly over her nose and mouth.

Flynn's men were prepared for Tru, but she was prepared for them.

My heart surges at the sight and I run toward her, ready to fight by her side.

Amethyst blurs into motion as he lures one of our attackers into Sage's line of sight. Without hesitation, Sage aims a marble at their temple and knocks them out cold.

Two of the five attackers are on the ground in seconds, but in another, there are more of them. They pour out of the tower and from the surrounding area and rush to surround us.

There are too many of them to track, too many to fight.

Tru is still too far away from me, and even as I drive my fist into a faceless attacker's jaw, I know that we are going to lose this fight.

I press on, and the next time I see Sage she's in Ryan's arms, a blade pressed against her neck.

"Stop!" he shouts.

I stop and so does everyone else.

"Sage!" It takes everything I have not to rush forward.

"Let her go!" Tru rips her mask down to be heard clearly.

"I would be happy to," Ryan says. "If you agree to go with me." He tips his head up, toward the top of the tower. "We could use your assistance with something."

Tru's hands turn into fists. Her eyes are pinned to Sage and her anger is palpable. Next to her, I feel utterly useless. After everything, I have nothing to offer. No way to help Tru in this moment. And no way to help my own sister.

"You do realize you're practically on top of Underhill, don't you?" Embry shouts. "All I have to do is—"

"What?" Ryan challenges. "Call your mother so she can come arrest Lila and let everyone else go? Because we both know that's what will happen. What can the toothless Boss Acosta do to Anderson Flynn?"

Embry grinds his teeth together and refuses to answer. Because the answer is nothing.

"I'll go," Tru says, her voice somehow soft and strong all at once. "Just let Sage go."

Ryan nods but presses the knife to Sage's neck a little harder as he drags her toward the base of the tower.

"Ouch!" Sage snaps. "You could have asked me to move, you know. I'm kind of actively not fighting you."

Ryan's lips twist in a wry smile because even in a situation like this, it's impossible not to find Sage absolutely endearing. Though I do wish she wouldn't antagonize her captor.

I have to smother the part of my mind that insists Ryan wouldn't hurt her—the part of me that thinks anything he showed me was real.

"Apologies, little sis," he says. "But I'm afraid this is part of the process. We'll do the exchange by the door, if you don't mind."

"I do mind, actually," Sage mutters, but she doesn't resist.

"Tru," I breathe, keeping my voice low enough that only she can hear. "She's alive. Anderson's daughter is alive and she's afraid."

"Anna," she says, turning to face me. "I figured it out when you asked for her number. Did you find her?"

I nod, but then shake my head.

"She doesn't want to come forward," Tru says, filling in the blanks. "I can't really blame her for that." She tips her head skyward, eyes locking on to Logan's distant form. "He won't give her up."

"He might if your life is in danger." I reach for her hand, wishing I could stop her from going up there. But we're out of options.

Tru nods, squeezing my hand as a glimmer of tears appear in her eyes. Then she throws her arms around me and pulls me against her. Part of me wants to hold her just like this forever. Or turn and run from all of this.

But the rest of me knows that isn't possible. Because there are so many people we love, and sometimes all we can do is the best right thing in the moment. Even if it feels like losing.

"Tell her to run," Tru whispers into my ear just before she pulls away and walks toward Ryan and Sage.

I push down the overwhelming surge of grief and helplessness, focusing instead on Tru and Sage as Ryan neatly exchanges one for the other. He's gone in an instant and Tru with him, the door at the base of the tower clanging shut as he yanks her inside.

The rest of the masked figures let Sage join me with Embry and Amethyst, but they don't make any move to disperse.

"Looks like we're all prisoners, then," Amethyst states.

I turn in a slow circle, getting a full picture of our situation for the first time. I estimate twenty people staged around us, with another six picking themselves up off the ground. It looks like overkill, even more so when you consider that half of us haven't graduated high school, but only until you consider that the most capable Enforcer in Underhill history is currently balanced at the top of the memorial tower.

"Any chance you can make a run for it and get out of here?" Embry asks, aiming the question at Amethyst.

Amethyst scans the crowd and shakes his head. "Not against five other wingtips. They'd box me in, in two seconds."

"So our only option is to sit down here like ducks while our best friend slash girlfriend is used as leverage against her own father?" Sage asks, though it's not really a question. "I have to say that I am feeling really angry right now."

"Me too," Amethyst volunteers, his voice deadly calm.

I look between the three of them and the sea of our faceless captors. At the bottom of the hill, Union Station is studded with light and, beneath it, the tunnels of Underhill.

Underhill claims to exist for moments like this—when talents decide that they can operate above any sense of law. But Ryan was right: Underhill would arrest me faster than it would someone like Anderson Flynn.

They don't know that I'm sitting up here. Practically gift wrapped for them.

But they could.

"I assume you all have your phones?" I ask, and when they nod, I smile. "Good. Because I need you all to report a sighting."

"A sighting of what?" Sage asks, eyes wide and unsuspecting.

"Of Lila Morgan."

The wingtips arrive first.

I count five of them. They ghost onto the scene, ready to claim their prize, but hesitate when they see the crowd. One of them turns away instantly and abandons the field. But the other four remain, and I guess I have the ridiculously high bounty to thank for that.

"Are you sure this was a good idea?" Sage asks, stepping in close to my side.

"I am," I say. "Isn't it straight from the Sage Morgan playbook?"

Embry laughs as he tucks himself into her other side. "I believe we call that administrative combat."

Sage huffs at that, but she can't deny that this is something she would do.

A squeal of tires announces yet more bounty hunters coming to try their hand at capturing a bombshell. Now there are twice as many people here as there were before my location was reported.

It's hard to say for sure with their faces blurred behind scrubbers, but I think Anderson Flynn's guards are starting to look a little nervous.

"What's the plan?" Amethyst asks as he presses his back to mine to complete our defensive square. "I assume there is one."

"We need to get up there." I lift my eyes toward the top of the tower. "So, I was thinking we'd just . . . fight in that general direction."

"They'll never see it coming," Embry says with utter sincerity.

"What if they catch you?" Sage asks.

It's a real possibility. Especially if Flynn's goons decide they'd really rather not deal with a bombshell and let the bounty hunters take care of me.

"We're not going to let that happen," Amethyst answers, surprising me with his vehemence. "Ready?"

In response, Sage issues a battle cry that splits the air and sends a shiver down my spine. I'm glad she's on my side as she expertly flings a handful of marbles at the figures closest to her, nailing five of them right between the eyes.

Amethyst blurs into motion and Embry dives ahead of me, carving the first steps of a path toward the base of the tower.

We have the smallest benefit of surprise before the entire world erupts into action around us.

I follow Embry, trading and dodging blows as they're aimed at me. But I'm fighting at a disadvantage.

Everyone else can use their talents.

There are too many people here. Too much potential for harm if I lose control for even a second, so I push the beat of my song down, down, down and let the others take more than their fair share of this fight. They created a shield around me, one on each side to prevent anyone from getting close enough to grab me as we inch toward the tower. Toward Tru and Logan.

The fight surges this way and that, pulling us away from our goal as frequently as it pushes us toward it. I have to focus on keeping my breathing even because everything inside of me wants to rush ahead. I want to let loose and mow down every obstacle between us and the door.

But I can't.

The longer we fight, the harder it is to hold even a modicum of calm. I am fission and panic and the tiniest spark will set me off. It is all I can think of.

The spark comes in the form of a cry from above.

Tru screams and it's a sound like no other. It resonates in my blood and sets every cell of my body alight with focus.

I look up in time to see Logan tip slowly backward off the high ledge. His broad shoulders blot out the stars above as he falls.

The Seventh Explosion of Lila Morgan

The world stills, but I am in motion. Moving faster than I should be able. Clearing the crowd. Stopping at the base of the tower and turning the volume up, up, up until the song soars through me, surges like the rush of water over a cliff. Rising and expanding in a single fluid motion.

I think of my father. Of the night he wrapped me in the shield of his arms. Of the way that felt inside and out.

And I explode.

There is a cushion of sound. Like being underwater but still able to hear the resonance of the world above the surface. Pressure squeezes in from all sides and my ears want to pop, and I feel the shimmering reverberation of sound in every part of my body.

Around me, the world has gone utterly still. I look up and for a second it's hard to process what I'm seeing. A body is suspended in the air only an arm's length above my head. Logan Dire rests there as though pillowed against something soft and supportive. Something that not only broke his fall, but is keeping him there.

And just above him, another figure.

Tru is there, too, suspended with her arms stretched toward her father, confusion and surprise clear on her face.

I am also surprised, but I am not confused. Because I can see what happened. Or, really, because I can feel what happened.

It's the song. *My* song, but instead of coursing through me, it's emanating from me. It isn't just rhythm and drive, but melody and harmony, and all of it responds to me. What I want and need. And what I want and need is to protect. Not destroy.

Just like my father.

The realization almost sucks the breath from my lungs.

Because he knew how to do this, too. He knew that a bombshell's talent could be wielded in more ways than one.

"You can let us down now, Lila." Logan's voice comes from just overhead.

There is a real difference between doing something instinctively and doing it intentionally. My whole body trembles with the sudden effort of *trying* to keep them afloat rather than just *doing* it, but I draw a steady, slow breath and focus on lowering them to the ground.

Logan touches down first. He looks worse than when I saw him earlier in the day, with dozens more bruises and cuts marking his face and arms, and that's just what I can see at a glance. The second his feet touch the ground, he reaches for Tru, gathering her in his arms as though he might never let her go again. It touches something brutal and raw inside me, and I have to look away.

I turn and find that even though it felt like we were very much alone here at the base of the tower, we are still surrounded.

There are nearly three dozen people here, staring at me. Every single one of them saw what I just did. Despite their facial scrubbers, I can feel their fear and awe, their distrust of me and every other bombshell they'll ever encounter.

But I think I might never be afraid of my own talents again.

The door at the base of the tower slams open and Ryan appears, breathing hard, like he raced to get here. His eyes are wide and pinned to me. Because he understands what just happened.

"Lila—" he gasps. "Are you—?"

"This is an executive order for disengagement! Stop what you're doing. Right now," a familiar voice rings out over the square, cutting off the rest of Ryan's question.

Boss Acosta approaches with a collection of Underhill Associates in signature gold and blue and black. She gestures and her team fans out around us. A few of our attackers flee, but most of them are too slow to get a jump on Boss Acosta's people.

Two Enforcers break away from the group and aim their steps for Ryan and for me. They're holding collars, which I can only assume are the evolution of my useless heart monitor. The one headed for Ryan knocks him to his knees before he clasps the collar around Ryan's neck. It hums like an engine powering up as it activates. It seems they added some extra features.

I take an involuntary step backward as the other Enforcer approaches me. Embry steps in front of me, and then so does Amethyst. Both of them ready to do battle.

"Mom!" Embry shouts. "She just saved their lives! You can't treat her like a criminal."

"It is a temporary measure, Embry," Boss Acosta answers. "And it's nonnegotiable."

Embry's hands fold into fists, but I put one hand on his shoulder. Not because I have any faith to put into Underhill, but because I have more than enough to put in my friends. "It's okay," I say.

"It's not," he grinds out, but he steps back.

The Enforcer steps between Embry and Amethyst to secure the collar around my neck. It snaps shut with an electric click and begins to hum.

I suspect it's meant to prevent me from using my talent, but I don't dare test it. Despite what I told Embry, this is bad.

"Thank you for your cooperation, Ms. Morgan." Boss Acosta doesn't look away from me as she moves deliberately up the stairs to the landing. Her entourage moves with her, spreading out behind her like wings.

"Ms. Acosta, may I ask why you are detaining my employees?"

Anderson Flynn strides into the center of the gathering. His hair is perfectly combed back, but there's a splatter of blood on his cheek. He's abandoned his suit jacket, and his sleeves are rolled up to the elbows, revealing muscled forearms. He looks like he was just in the middle of something messy, which I assume is because he was.

"For the unsanctioned kidnapping of an Underhill Associate," Boss Acosta states bluntly.

I'm just as surprised as Mr. Flynn, who seems to be at a temporary loss for words.

"What proof do you have?" he demands.

"I've had a very thorough statement from a source who shall remain anonymous until it is both appropriate and safe to reveal their identity, per Underhill regulations," Boss Acosta says. "I'd also like to have a conversation with Ms. Morgan about the circumstances of her recent absence. Do you have a problem with that?"

His look of pure rage says that he does have a problem with that, but he gives a single tight shake of his head.

"Good, then there's one more thing—"

"Yes, there is," Anderson says, cutting her off. "I am here to formally accuse Logan Dire of the murder of my daughter, Simone Flynn. He has all but admitted it already—we always assumed that he was lying when he said there were other people there that night, but we were never able to prove it. I demand that Underhill get to the bottom of this and seek justice for my daughter."

"I couldn't agree with you more, Mr. Flynn." Boss Acosta steps forward like a lioness, with power and patience and the utmost confidence that her prey has just walked into her trap. "In fact, I was just having the most interesting conversation about this very matter."

She tips her head to the side and Anna Mirth steps forward, her hands clasped firmly before her, jaw set as she stares directly into her father's disbelieving face.

"Simone." He breathes the word, and it's delightful to

watch as all his plans come crashing down in a single second.

"Father," she answers, and by contrast her voice sounds firm, as if she just packed years of fear and resentment into that one word.

"I think we'll have this all cleared up very soon, don't you?" Boss Acosta asks, and continues without waiting for a response. "Ms. Grey, Mr. Dire, I'm glad to see you're both well. I expect you both to report to Underhill within the hour to give statements. I understand we have a lot of ground to cover to unravel all of this."

"We'll come together," Logan says, one arm still wrapped around Tru's shoulders. Protective, but also a united front.

"Mr. Flynn, would you come with me, please." Boss Acosta gestures down the steps to where a fleet of black sedans waits on the drive.

Mr. Flynn is still glaring at his daughter, but Anna ignores him. She tips her head in my direction in silent acknowledgment. I'm glad for her. Worried, too, but mostly glad. At least now she can live without constantly worrying that she'll be found.

"I do mean now, Mr. Flynn," Boss Acosta adds in a steely voice.

Mr. Flynn clears his throat and strides forward as though this were all his idea. As though he isn't being very lightly arrested in front of all these witnesses.

"Mom!" Embry shouts.

Boss Acosta spins on her heel and comprehends his

question before he can say another word. She smiles at me. "It's temporary, like I said, but I understand it isn't comfortable. I assume I can trust you to arrive with Mr. Dire and Ms. Grey?"

"Yes, ma'am," I say.

That seems to be enough for Boss Acosta. She turns, gesturing to her guards with one hand, and they follow with Anderson secure between them.

As soon as they're gone, my friends swallow me whole. I'm dimly aware that Logan has taken a few steps back to give us space. They surround me with eight arms, our heads crashing together as some of us laugh and Sage definitely cries a little. It's like being wrapped inside a cloud, stuffy and hot and soft, and after a few minutes, it's too much and we disentangle our limbs.

"I'd say let's never do anything like this again, but I'm pretty sure that's tempting fate," Sage says, wiping her eyes. "I mean, I have no idea if I believe in fate, but I'm beginning to suspect it believes in us."

"That's nonsense," Embry says, pulling her against him so she can use his shirt as a tissue.

"You're nonsense," she mutters in response.

"Mostly," he agrees.

"Agreed," Amethyst adds. "Except I think you're both nonsense."

Tru takes advantage of their distraction to step closer. "Are you hurt?" she asks, eyes skimming over my face.

"Me?" I shake my head. "You're the one who threw yourself off the top of a very tall tower just now. But I assume you're not hurt."

"Good as ever," she says with a nod. Her eyes drop to my lips, and heat stirs in my belly. "I'd like to formally request a do-over."

"What?" I ask, the heat now driving up into my cheeks, my thoughts stuck on the fizzy desire to press my lips to hers.

"A do-over," she repeats, that sweet smile of hers making it hard to think. "Of our date. Would you like to?"

"I would," I answer, aware that my voice is more breath than tone.

"Great," she says, smile widening. She catches my hand, and together we join our friends, and Logan, each of us taking a minute to enjoy that we're together. Safe.

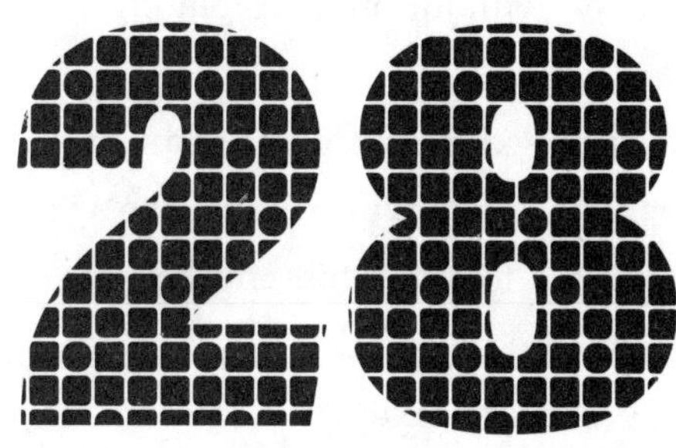

I arrive at the Stallard house exactly when Sage told me to. Six thirty on the dot. I don't even have a chance to knock before the door sweeps open and Sage greets me with a "Good evening, Miss. Do you have a reservation?"

She's dressed for the part in a simple black top, black slacks, and a black apron tied around her waist.

"I . . . do?" I guess.

"Name, please?" she continues, checking an invisible appointment book in her empty hands.

"Sage," I say with mild exasperation.

"No Sage on this list," she muses. I take a steadying breath and hold my ground until finally she rolls her eyes at me. "All right, all right. Table for two? Right this way."

Sage leads me through the living room toward the kitchen. The place looks practically the same as when I lived here. Which is mostly a reflection of how bad I was at settling in. The only real change is that there is a pair of men's running shoes in the small collection by the front door and a stack of fantasy novels on the table by the comfy chair.

A lot has changed in the weeks since the Anderson Flynn incident. Flynn was exiled from all Underhill protections and alliances. I had hoped for more, but since he had only *attempted* to have his daughter murdered, there wasn't much they could do to him. He was sent home without much ceremony and that was that.

The thing that really surprised me was that Ryan chose to stay. After all that effort trying to convince me to take a job with Flynn, he decided to tithe to Underhill and become a sanctioned Associate.

The day he made his decision, he texted me:

> *If I stay in your city, are we destined to be enemies?*

I knew he was really asking whether or not I was still angry with him for all that had happened between us. I was, but I also wasn't.

I answered, **Only when we're chasing the same bounties.**

I can live with that.

I still don't trust him, exactly, but we work well together. We'd spent hours figuring out how to replicate the protective effect I'd used to save Logan and Tru. Once I'd understood the mechanism, it was easy to teach, and Ryan was a quick study. After several public demonstrations and more than a few impassioned speeches from my friends, we even convinced Underhill to disband the Bombshell Containment Task Force.

Not only had I been reinstated as an Underhill Associate, but I'd been offered a promotion.

That had soothed my bank account enough that I could find a new apartment of my own. I appreciated the free lodging at Tru's house, but it was just too much to cohabitate with the person I was also trying to date. Sage technically moved with me, but she spends more nights over here than she does with me.

Still, as I follow Sage into the warmth of the kitchen, I feel a twinge of loss. I had spent my mornings here doing my best not to disturb Tru as she finished her baking, grabbing a cup of tea before hurrying out the door, and my evenings hovering off to the side while the core group of friends made dinner together. I'd been so worried about disturbing their balance that I hadn't realized how much I enjoyed being with them in this space.

"We have a truly spectacular menu planned for this evening," Sage says as we cross the floor toward the little table. It's been swathed in a red tablecloth, decorated with long taper candles, and dusted with pretty pink petals that must have come from a carnation. "Do you have any allergies I should be aware of?" she asks.

"Yes, I'm allergic to sage," I say, but my eyes are locked on Tru.

She's already seated but stands to meet me, a shy smile on her lips. Her hair has been styled into big, soft curls that rest on her shoulders, and she's wearing a green blouse that turns the mosaic of her eyes more green than brown.

"I'm going to ignore that comment and give you two a minute to decide on your drinks," Sage chirps as she backs away.

"Hey," Tru says.

"Hi," I answer, reaching for her hand. "Has she been like this all day?"

A little laugh brightens Tru's smile. "She has, but wait until you see Logan. I think he's even more all in than Sage."

"I find that utterly unbelievable."

She draws me toward the table and we sink into our chairs, which have been arranged so that we're next to each other rather than across the table.

"I think Sage has infected him with something," Tru says.

I give a solemn nod. "I've seen it before. And I'm sorry to say it will probably get worse before it gets better."

"I think this whole thing," she says, gesturing to the world in general, "changed him a bit. And I mean more than his new limp."

Logan had recovered from the injuries inflicted by Anderson Flynn and his people. The damage to his leg was a few months older. It had happened in this very kitchen, when he exploded a giant sack of flour to allow Tru to escape.

From me.

He'd only survived because the Saint decided not to kill

him. That revelation had set us all reeling; it was hard to accept that the person who'd had us running for our lives was the very person who had saved Logan's. But, years earlier, Logan had left the Saint alive and, as Logan put it, "Sometimes a debt is more important than a bounty."

"I'm glad they've found a way to connect. With Sage, you kind of have to submit to the effervescence or let it destroy you."

"I can still hear you!" Sage calls from just outside the kitchen.

"Why are you still here?!" I shout back.

"Because—"

She's cut off by a sudden rush of noise, notably Embry's voice asking her to take something, and Amethyst's telling him they could have made two trips if he didn't always think like a strongarm.

In another minute, they appear in the doorway bearing a feast between the three of them—a bowl of beautiful salad, plates of roasted vegetables and meat, along with a basket of freshly baked bread.

"Dinner is served," Sage announces as the three of them arrange everything on the table before us.

"It looks amazing," Tru says with admiration.

"Logan was in charge of the dessert, and I know he's excited to share it with you when you're ready for it," Sage says.

"How could you tell he was excited?" Embry asks.

"Oh, I could tell," Sage says. "We have a *connection*, you know."

"Does *he* know?" Amethyst teases.

"He knows." Logan is suddenly there, standing directly behind Sage, who is the only one who doesn't jump at his surprise appearance.

I have to laugh at the look on their faces. And then I'm laughing for another reason.

I am happy. Deeply, undeniably happy to be, in this kitchen, surrounded by people I like more than a little bit.

"I have to be honest," Embry says with a wicked smile on his face. "It's kind of unnerving when she laughs."

"It usually precedes something much more dangerous," Sage adds.

"Okay," Tru says, standing up and pointing toward the front of the house. "You are all marvelous, loving humans and we are very grateful for this amazing dinner, but you are currently crashing our fourth date, so . . ."

"We're going!" Sage hops up and spins to usher the others ahead of her. "And we won't be back until your curfew!"

"Are you kidding right now?" I call.

"She's kidding," Logan says, turning for one final look at the two of us. "I'll be back before that."

He says it with such sincerity that even knowing it's a joke, I still feel it as a threat.

We've only just dished out our salads when our phones buzz.

We lock eyes, neither one of us wanting to be the first one to check. So we do it together.

"Should we?" Tru asks, phone in hand.

"Sage will kill us," I answer, already swiping into the app, where a new bounty waits.

"Yeah." Tru sighs. "But only a little."

There's a beat of silence and our eyes lock, but there's no denying what we both want. Maybe dating is never going to be a thing Tru and I manage to do. And maybe we are just redefining what dating means to us. The same way we've had to redefine what our talents mean to us, what family means to us. Maybe the important part about dating is simply doing things together. And we are nailing that part. I smile and tap to open the bounty while Tru does the same. When we look up again, the decision has already been made.

"Let's do it."

Acknowledgments

This is a story that I got wrong before I got it right. When I wrote the first draft, I started in Tru's point of view, thinking it was her story. I got all the way to the climactic final scenes before I realized that I couldn't tell this story without Lila's help. But I was up against a deadline, and instead of owning up to my mistake, I peppered Lila's point of view throughout the manuscript, hoping it would be enough to convince my editor (and, if I'm being honest, myself) that it was meant to be a story told from two points of view.

It was not. And my editor was very kind when she pointed out that the telling of this story belonged to Lila and asked if I would like to try again. So, first and foremost, my thanks to Miriam Newman, who is a talent of the finest order—the bulls-eye of editing! Thank you for always seeing the story as clearly as I do and for helping me tell or retell it, as the case may be.

I am also immensely grateful to the entire Candlewick team for making so much of the invisible work that goes into publishing novels feel nearly effortless. Thank you to Natalie Bricker, Sarah Chaffee Paris, Jackie Houton, Maria Middleton, Nathan Pyritz, Carolynn DeCillo, Sarah Sherman,

Erin DeWitt, Neda Kamalhedayat, and my Walker UK editor, Ruth Knowles! Thank you also to cover artist Jonathan Bartlett for creating another perfect fit for these characters.

Thanks as always to my agent, Lara Perkins, and her assistant, Audrey Mueller, for helping me navigate schedules and contracts so I can focus on writing. Thanks also to my friends—especially to Alys, Dhonielle, Zoraida, and Tara—for helping me navigate the other difficult parts of publishing so I can keep writing. Thanks double especially to my husband, Tessa, for helping me navigate the difficult parts of writing so I can tell the story.

Finally, thank you, my readers, for returning to Underhill, Inc., and following Lila and Tru on another adventure.